ZUTO
THE ADVENTURES OF
A COMPUTER
VIRUS

Udi Aharoni

Illustrations: Gil Troitsa

Translated into English by: Amit Pardes
English version edited by: Lior Betzer
Thanks to Dr. Ellen Schur and to Cindy Kane for additional editing and useful comments.

ISBN-13: 978-1477683309
ISBN-10: 1477683305

Dedicated with love to my parents, my brother, and his family.

All software programs appearing in this work are fictitious. Any resemblance to real software is purely coincidental. The Zutopedia appendix explains the truth behind the story.

Chapter 1

The story you are about to read is extraordinary: it is only one minute long, and it takes place in an area no larger than several square millimeters. This may be a world record, and the author certainly means to look into it. Anyway, the reason that an entire story is compressed into such limited measures of space and time is because it takes place inside a computer, and in a computer, one square millimeter is an entire world, and one minute is almost eternity.

The story takes place during one perfectly normal and hot summer afternoon, and the computer in question is owned by a boy named Tom. If you asked Tom what happened during that hot afternoon, he'd probably frown in confusion and say that nothing happened. His computer did act a little weird at the time, and Tom noticed it and was surprised, but, as we just said, it was only for one minute, after which the computer went back to its normal behavior.

It all started because a computer virus had infiltrated Tom's computer, a virus quite similar to the type known as "Zutrog-33." His friends called him Zuto.

Let's now dive into Tom's computer, twenty-seven seconds after five past three on a hot summer afternoon. This is precisely when our one-minute story begins, and we land in the center of the Mathematical Co-Processor.

The Mathematical Co-Processor was a moderately-sized city, and at the time, it was bustling as usual. Numbers streamed into the city, gracefully sliding on shiny cables, one bit after the other. (A bit is the numeral zero or one. Numerals 2-9 aren't used in the computer. You can read more in the Zutopedia at the end of the book.) Its thousands of residents filled the streets and factories, going about their business at a leisurely pace (don't be surprised that things occur slowly within the computer; we've slowed down the passage of time so that we can observe what was happening, but in fact, a worker can cross the entire city before you have time to blink), pushing wheelbarrows full of bits around and operating all sorts of devices.

The anti-virus, Silver Shield, a silver metal robot, glided on a motorcycle as shiny as himself into the city's main street. That wasn't an ominous sign, just a routine patrol. Suddenly, Silver Shield noticed graffiti painted in black letters on the wall of one of the houses. "HELP," it read. Silver Shield parked his bike, got off, and walked towards the suspicious inscription in order to examine it closely.

He was a tall and strong anti-virus, with a huge sword hanging diagonally across his back covered by a silver shield. Workers who walked down the street, pushing their wheelbarrows, gazed at him curiously but kept a safe distance.

While studying the graffiti on the wall, Silver Shield noticed a second inscription out of the corner of his eye, down a nearby alley. "Help! Over here!" read the second inscription painted in the same black letters. *Is there some sort of danger that requires my attention?* the anti-virus wondered as he entered the alley, his heavy metal feet pounding. The graffiti went on along the wall: "Help! I'm further down!" "Just a bit more . . ." "You're almost there . . ." Silver Shield continued walking and reading. At the end of the alley he read the last inscription out loud: "I am now stealing your motorcycle."

He turned his head towards the main road and indeed, on his motorcycle sat a small green figure: Zuto.

Zuto perched on the silver motorcycle and tried, unsuccessfully, to start the engine. He turned his eyes towards the alley and saw Silver Shield looking right back at him. The little virus realized that the chase had begun and that he should quickly find the right handle and take off.

Silver Shield recovered and started running back toward the road. While he ran, he drew his sword from the sheath hanging across his back, moving with tremendous speed for such a large anti-virus. Zuto had already caused him many problems in the past, and seeing him sitting now in bewildered confusion on his motorcycle, Silver Shield thought that this was a perfect opportunity to exterminate the little pest, once and for all.

He increased his speed, raised his sword high in the air with both hands, and prepared for a crushing blow. Then he leapt and forcefully swung down the sword.

A clang of metal disturbed the peaceful city. The sharp sword barely missed Zuto's head and hit the ground because just then, the virus found the accelerator grip and took off with a roar. He sped away as fast as he could, which was pretty fast, considering he had never ridden a motorcycle before, and tried to navigate among the workers and their wheelbarrows. The heavy pounding of Silver Shield's pursuing feet echoed in his ears, but steadily grew fainter and fainter, and Zuto started to taste victory.

Just then, the road curved sharply into another street that led out of the city. Zuto, smiling triumphantly, suddenly found himself face to face with a worker hauling a wheelbarrow laden with bits. The startled worker abandoned his wheelbarrow and jumped for cover between two houses on the side of the road, while Zuto sharply wrenched the handlebar to the other side. The motorcycle slid into the wheelbarrow, and Zuto, the motorcycle, the wheelbarrow, and the bits in it flew in all directions and scattered on the street.

"Are you crazy?" yelled the worker, who quickly regained his senses and returned to the middle of the road. "Don't you know how to drive?!"

"I apologize," said Zuto. "I don't have much experience riding a motorcycle."

He got back on to his feet and wiped the dust off his body. "Here, let me help you put those bits back in the wheelbarrow," he added, and started gathering the scattered bits.

The two quickly completed the task, and the wheelbarrow was full again and ready to go. (Because of the commotion, the bits were now piled in the wrong order, which caused a calculation error. The city's workers were busy dividing the number 4195835 by the number 3145727, and the mess on the wheelbarrow caused the result to be 1.333739068902037589 instead of 1.333820449136241002.) Only then did the worker lift his eyes and got a good look at Zuto.

"Virus!" he shrieked and leapt to hide by the side of the road again. From the direction of the main road, Silver Shield's pounding footsteps could be heard again, drawing closer. Zuto didn't hesitate. He jumped on the motorcycle and fled the scene. The worker waited in his hiding place until the virus disappeared over the horizon, and only then did he venture out, pick up the handles of his wheelbarrow, and start marching, mumbling, "Really, how can one get any work done this way?"

Just then, Silver Shield appeared around the corner and ran straight towards the wheelbarrow. He crashed into it, overturned it, and fell down, taking the poor worker with him.

Chapter 2

Tom was completely unaware of Zuto's presence, since Silver Shield still had not informed him of Zuto's existence. The damages caused by the little virus weren't significant, and so far hadn't disrupted the computer's normal function. (Take, for example, the error caused by the accident in the Mathematical Co-Processor. It merely caused a button in one of the windows on the screen to move one millimeter to the left from its original location.)

While the events in the Mathematical Co-Processor took place, Tom finished downloading and installing a new movie player, Super Media 3.0. He wasn't happy with his previous movie player, Super Media 2.0, which stalled, skipped, and stuttered when playing movies due to what the manufacturer's site called a "known bug in this version."

Meanwhile, inside the computer, Zuto rode away smugly on the shiny motorcycle to his hiding place: the Recycle Bin. The Recycle Bin was a distant open area in which mountains and mountains of garbage had accumulated with time. There were huge piles of boxes and paper files and books and old pictures and all sorts of odd items, as well as several old and defective software applications that shared their residence with Zuto and knew him well.

Zuto rode into the center of the Recycle Bin. There, among the mountains of garbage, stretched a small field full of wild weeds. When he arrived, he was surprised to see a small, unfamiliar figure sitting on a ramshackle brown wooden box on the edge of the field, crying. The figure was so absorbed in its tears that it didn't even notice the motorcycle that stopped beside it. Zuto waited, embarrassed, hoping it would notice him, stop crying, and raise its head. When that didn't happen, he faintly cleared his throat. The figure lifted its head and looked at him.

"Virus!" she screamed, jumping up and standing on the box. Now Zuto could see her clearly. She was tall and pretty. A black celluloid ribbon wound its way around her body like a dress. An abundance of long, thin celluloid ribbons flowed from her head to her shoulders and back. Her green eyes looked at him fearfully.

"Allow me to assure you, lady," said Zuto, "that I have no intention of harming you. Please don't be afraid."

"H-h-how can I trust you?" she asked, "after all . . . you are a v-virus. Although I must admit that I've never met a virus before, and I cer-certainly wouldn't expect him to be so p-polite."

Even though she was afraid, she spoke with a serenity and confidence that surprised Zuto.

"I've never met a virus before, either," he said thoughtfully, "other than myself, of course, so I don't really know how they normally behave. For my part, I try not to harm anyone."

"Isn't that Silver Shield's motorcycle?" she asked suddenly. Everyone knew Silver Shield and his famous motorcycle.

"Uhhh . . . yeah." Zuto shrugged.

"There you go!" she said, "you s-stole his motorcycle. From which I can conclude that you are ha-ha-harmful and not nice at all."

"Well," replied Zuto, "of course I'm not nice to Silver Shield. He's been trying to eliminate me for some time now, so why should I be nice to him?"

The figure thought to herself that Zuto had a point and pondered whether it was enough to justify his actions.

"That aside," Zuto added, "surely you know that standing on a box does not give you any kind of immunity against viruses."

"I'm afraid I must agree with you on that matter," she said, and climbed off the box. "I'm used to people climbing up on an elevated object when they are alarmed by something. That's how it is in the movies."

"So who are you really?" he asked now that she was standing closer to him.

"I'm Super Media 2.0," she said and lowered her gaze. "I was just cast aside because of Su- because of Su-" she took a deep breath, "because of Super Media 3.0."

"Oh, right," said Zuto, "you've been replaced with a newer version."

"Yes, because I stut-stut-stutter," she confessed. Tears gathered in her eyes again.

Zuto didn't know what to say, so he just let her cry quietly.

Super Media 2.0 took a deep breath and asked, "So why did you steal the mo-motorcycle? Apart from your general intention to irritate Silver Shield?"

Zuto had never stopped to think about it, until now. Of course, in his opinion, any deed that could annoy Silver Shield was a worthy one, yet he had many other easier and simpler ways to irritate the anti-virus. So why did he choose to put himself at risk by stealing the motorcycle?

"I kept seeing Silver Shield ride this motorcycle," he finally said, "and I saw everyone looking at him with respect and clearing the way for him. I envied him. I thought that if I borrowed the motorcycle and rode it, I would feel big and important too. Anyway, I intend to return it soon."

Super Media 2.0 was impressed by his honest answer. "Well," she asked, "Did you feel big and important when you rode over here?"

"Yes," admitted Zuto, "I felt different. The wind on my face . . . the rumble of the engine beneath me . . . just for a moment I forgot that I'm nothing but a small, green creature and I felt as though I was . . . someone!"

While he spoke, Super Media 2.0 kept drawing closer to the motorcycle. Red and blue buttons protruded from the dashboard.

"I wonder what this button is for," said Zuto and pressed the blue button. A small light up front started flickering blue, and the loud sound of a siren sliced the air. Zuto jumped off the motorcycle in alarm and landed upside down in one of the garbage piles.

Super Media 2.0 laughed. "It's only a siren," she said, turning it off by pushing the blue button again. "What startled you so?"

Embarrassed, Zuto got up and stood by her again. "I'm used to running away when I hear that sound," he explained. "It's instinctive."

They looked at each other and suddenly both of them burst out laughing.

"Now let's check what the red button is for," said Zuto and reached out.

"Are you crazy?" cried Super Media 2.0. She stopped his hand before he could press the button.

"What?" Zuto asked in wonder.

"Red buttons are dangerous. That's how it is in the movies."

"Come on," said Zuto, "don't be such a scaredy-cat."

"I *am* a scaredy-cat," confessed Super Media 2.0 proudly. "That's how I protect myself from danger."

"You don't . . ." Zuto tried to continue arguing, but just then, Newton, an old friend of his, stepped into the field.

Chapter 3

Newton was the name of a simple software application that performed mathematical operations, like a calculator. In the past, Newton had served Tom well, but once, a long time ago, the application had suddenly gone crazy and simply stopped performing the calculations it was asked to do. It seemed as though it had become absorbed in calculations of its own. Tom decided to delete it and threw it in the Recycle Bin.

Newton looked around and climbed up on the box that Super Media 2.0 had stood on just a short while ago. He resembled a square, bluish calculator.

"Hear ye, hear ye!" Newton cried and waved his short arms as he gazed out to the center of the field, pretending it was packed with a crowd that had come to hear him speak.

"Who's he talking to?" whispered Super Media 2.0, who stood beside Zuto on the edge of the field.

"He's a bit crazy," explained Zuto. "He has this subject that he really likes talking about. You'll hear about it in a moment."

"Hear ye, hear ye!" Newton repeated with much pathos, waving his arms again, "and I shall tell you about the greatest scientific discovery in history, discovered by yours truly." He looked around the empty field as if to gauge the crowd's reaction.

"Once," he continued loudly, "I was wandering about, preoccupied with my work. As I passed under one of the cables, a bit broke off and fell on my head . . ."

Newton paused in order to take a deep breath. "And then suddenly I realized," he continued, "that these bits are the foundations of everything, everything that is happening here—it all begins with them."

"Is it true, what he's saying?" Super Media 2.0 whispered to Zuto. I don't get it."

"I have dedicated much time to observing these bits," continued Newton, "and to all that happens to them in various factories, and I have gradually formed my ideas into a simple, beautiful theory."

"I think it's true," Zuto answered, even though he didn't really get it either, "but I never actually checked it myself."

"I call my theory 'Mathematical Principles of Nature,'" Newton continued. "It contains several simple mathematical formulas of Boolean algebra. The entire world operates according to these formulas—"

"Newton?" Zuto interrupted.

"Yes?" said Newton. "Is there a question in the crowd? Who's asking?"

"Umm, it's me," said Zuto, raising his hand. "Did you see my new motorcycle?"

To Zuto's relief, Newton was intrigued enough to cut short his speech. "Hmmm," he mumbled, jumping off the box and approaching them.

"Silver Shield's bike," he said. "Isn't it?"

"Yes," said Zuto proudly.

Newton fondled the motorbike. "May I dismantle it?" he asked.

"I don't think so," said Super Media 2.0, "that's Silver Shield's mo-motorcycle and we have to return it intact."

"What a shame," Newton said in disappointment. "I wanted to check if this motorcycle works according to the principles of my theory. If so, the theory would receive significant support. I yearn for the moment when I shall publicly present my theory and gain recognition as a distinguished scientist—" He stopped talking suddenly and peeked at Super Media 2.0.

"Who is she?" he whispered to Zuto.

"That's Super Media 2.0," answered Zuto, "she's new here."

Super Media 2.0 looked at the two of them whispering. Newton's disappointment moved her. "Isn't there a way to support your theory," she asked, "without van-vandalizing Silver Shield's property?"

"Hmmm," Newton hummed and started pacing the field, deep in thought.

"I had an idea," Zuto suddenly said. "I thought about it on the way over here: to jump over the Firewall with the motorcycle."

"Great idea!" Newton's face brightened. "I can calculate the speed required for takeoff, the trajectory of the flight, the point of impact, and the strike velocity using my theory!"

"I'm not sure if that's such a great idea," Super Media 2.0 said in concern. "Silver Shield might get mad."

"She's a worrier," Zuto explained to Newton. "I think she's something of a scaredy-cat."

"And proud of it," said Super Media 2.0.

"Ma'am," said Newton importantly, "in the name of science, we must take risks." He went off to rummage through a nearby pile of garbage. "This will do perfectly," he said, lifting something that he found under a battered kettle and a pile of Easter eggs (see Zutopedia). It was a long, flat board. Newton hoisted it on his shoulder and walked over to the box that served as his speaker's platform. "This too," he said. "Yes, these two will do to build a ramp."

Zuto and Newton got on the bike.

"Will you join us?" Zuto asked Super Media 2.0, who stood back and watched them. "There's room for one more."

"Where are you going?" she asked.

"Port 80," answered Newton.

"I'm not sure if I feel so co-comfortable with your plans," said Super Media 2.0, climbing on the motorcycle, "but I don't want to stay here by my-myself."

Zuto turned the accelerator grip, and the three were on their way.

Chapter 4

At one of the edges of the world lay a deep, wide blue sea. Hundreds of ports have been built along the coast, but the most beautiful and impressive one was Port 80 (see Zutopedia), which lay inside a natural bay surrounded by white shores and, beyond, wild green meadows. The elongated harbor, full of cranes and heavy machinery, was on the side of the bay. Bits meant to be shipped overseas were transported on cables into a large warehouse next to the harbor, where they waited to be loaded on one of the outbound ships. Other cables transported back inland bits unloaded from the incoming ships. Along the coast, guarding the port entrance, wound a gigantic wall of fire. Many dangers lurk at sea, but the flames of the Firewall (see Zutopedia) surged high and glowed far and wide, sending a clear warning message: Enter at your own risk.

On the other side of the bay was a small hill, overlooking the port. Zuto stopped the bike at its edge. Beyond the hill, they could see the Firewall, glowing and singeing the sky with its flames, and behind it, the tip of a green and white lighthouse, which was perched on a tiny rocky island. A large, illuminated sign spun slowly at the top, reading: "Port 80."

Three ships were moored in the harbor, and just as the group arrived there, one ship broke away and starting sailing towards the open sea. Zuto and his friends watched it glide upon the water and pause by the Firewall. It sounded its horn.

"Will the Firewall let it pass?" wondered Zuto.

"We'll see in a moment," answered Newton. "The Firewall's job is to prevent the entrance of dangerous things into our world through the ports, but it's also in charge of preventing the illegal smuggling of information out of our world. This ship is sailing to another computer, carrying a cargo of bits. The Firewall is now examining the cargo, who sent it, and where it is going. We'll soon see the results of the inspection."

Suddenly, a crack appeared in the Firewall, and then a wide gate opened slowly, allowing passage to the sea. The ship sailed through the gate and started its journey. The gate closed immediately after it had passed.

"What a spectacular sight," breathed Super Media 2.0. "Until now, I've been so ab-absorbed in my work that I didn't have time to en-enjoy the wonders of our world."

"And now, the experiment!" shouted Newton suddenly and started pacing the hill, carrying out calculations. Various numbers flickered on his screen, and he waved his hands about.

"Here, this is the exact location," he finally said, standing near the hill's summit. He put down the box and the board he had brought with him from the Recycle Bin, and constructed a small ramp facing the lighthouse.

"If you accelerate up the hill using all of the motorcycle's power and ride up the ramp," he explained to Zuto as he demonstrated with his hand, "the motorcycle will fly over the Firewall, and land, according to my calculations, right at the top of the lighthouse."

"Great," Zuto said excitedly and hurried to the bottom of the incline.

"This looks really dangerous," Super Media 2.0 said worriedly, walking towards the ramp in order to examine the ramshackle box's stability.

"Don't worry," Zuto yelled, already seated on the motorcycle at the bottom of the hill, "I always land on my feet. . . ."

Zuto gazed straight ahead towards the lighthouse and prepared to perform his stunt. His heart pounded loudly. He took a deep breath and turned the accelerator grip of the motorcycle with all his strength. The motorcycle galloped forward, gaining speed on its way up the hill, climbed the ramp, and leapt into the air.

Several porters, who had been unloading one of the ships on the other side of the bay, now froze and stared in astonishment at the unusual sight: a small, greenish figure riding a silver motorcycle, crossing the sky over the Firewall. One porter was so amazed that he dropped the rope that he was holding, and one of the cranes toppled into the water, dragging with it the entire content of the ship (the bits that it contained were actually a picture destined for Tom's browser. He had opened an Internet page describing the features of his new media player, Super Media 3.0, but now the only thing to appear in place of the company logo would be a red X indicating a missing picture).

Zuto landed exactly on top of the lighthouse, on the pad where the illuminating sign was installed. He circled the pad several times and stopped.

"Hurray!" Newton shouted. He jumped up and down and waved his hands in the air. "My mathematical principles actually work in practice!"

"Amazing," admitted Super Media 2.0, and clapped her hands loudly.

Zuto turned to face them and raised his arms in victory.

Silver Shield, whose motorcycle had been stolen, wandered around on foot, searching for trails, when he suddenly saw, at a distance, his motorcycle flying over the Firewall. He broke into a run and climbed up the hill, grim-faced, totally ignoring Newton and Super Media 2.0. When he reached the summit he stood and looked at the lighthouse.

"Zuto," he called in a calm but firm voice, "turn yourself in immediately! Bring back my motorcycle, or I will issue an order to blow up the lighthouse."

Zuto had no intention of turning himself in. He had meant to return the motorcycle anyway, but now he had to do it without getting caught. He squeezed the handle, and once again, the motorcycle flew over the Firewall and landed on top of the hill, next to Silver Shield.

Zuto didn't stop, but continued zooming down the hill at breakneck speed. The furious anti-virus started chasing him, the pounding of his feet echoing down the hill. Suddenly, Zuto braked while turning the handlebars sharply to the left. The motorcycle swerved sharply, kicking up a large amount of weeds and dust, and stalled. Zuto jumped off the bike and stood behind it just as Silver Shield arrived. Now the motorcycle lay in the middle, with Silver Shield on one side and Zuto on the other.

The two stared at each other intensely.

"Will he ki-ki-" Super Media 2.0 wanted to ask Newton, but had a hard time completing the sentence. Both of them stood at a safe distance and watched the unfolding drama. She took a deep breath and continued, "kill Zuto?"

"No," Newton said and waved his hands scornfully, "Zuto's too quick for him."

The silver robot looked huge next to green, little Zuto. He started running around the motorcycle and Zuto started running as well, so that they remained opposite each other. Then, the anti-virus suddenly changed course, and started running in the opposite direction. Zuto didn't lose even one clock cycle (see Zutopedia) and started running nimbly in the opposite direction as well, and once again, the two remained opposite each other.

Silver Shield realized that the entire matter was pointless and stood still.

"When will you realize that the computer isn't your own private playground?" he asked Zuto.

"So whose playground is it?" Zuto responded.

"It isn't a playground at all!" Silver Shield fumed.

Zuto smiled, intending to retort, when suddenly a strange rumble rolled in from the sea. The Firewall started quivering. It lost its altitude; its flames paled, and then they extinguished and disappeared completely. The wide sea was revealed in all its glory.

"Zuto!" yelled Silver Shield, "what did you do now?"

"It wasn't me," protested Zuto. "I was here the entire time. I wouldn't know how to make a Firewall disappear, even if I wanted to."

The sturdy anti-virus looked concerned. He rushed back to the top of the hill to get a better look. Then he pulled a walkie-talkie from his belt and started speaking anxiously.

Newton and Super Media 2.0 joined Zuto, who was still standing at the bottom of the hill.

"How strange that a Firewall should suddenly crash for no apparent reason," said Newton.

Silver Shield returned and stood next to them.

"Okay, it really does have nothing to do with you, Zuto," he admitted. "I checked with the Operating System guys" (see Zutopedia). "It's their fault. They're handling the matter urgently and promised that soon the Firewall will be reactivated.

"They've had too many failures lately," he mumbled to himself quietly.

"And in the meantime?" asked Super Media 2.0, "aren't we ex-exposed to the da-dangers of the sea?"

"We are exposed," answered Silver Shield. "The firewall has crashed all over, and all ports are defenseless. Let's hope that there won't be any serious damage until the matter is taken care of."

The four of them sat on the grass and watched the open sea, waiting for the moment when the flames guarding the bay's entrance would rise. Suddenly, the calm blue waters stretching to the horizon seemed ominous. Time crawled by slowly in tense silence.

The porters in the harbor resumed working as usual. Had they stopped working, the warehouse would have filled up and the bits streaming to it would have been thrown away. One of the two ships left in the harbor stood empty after its cargo had spilled by mistake into the water, and now they were busy repainting the inscription on its side in order to send it off to a new destination. The second ship was almost fully loaded.

A loud roll of thunder was heard, and the Firewall flared up again. Its flames quickly rose to their original height and resumed their glowing, healthy shine.

"Very good," Silver Shield said in relief, a smile on his face. Newton and Zuto clapped cheerfully.

The loaded ship broke free from its mooring and started sailing out.

"Let's s-stay and watch another ship sail to sea," said Super Media 2.0. "It's so pretty and peaceful."

Everyone agreed and stayed put. Suddenly, a huge explosion was heard from the heart of the bay, the ship shuddered, and it went up in flames. The four of them sprang to their feet in alarm.

"Oh, no!" Super Media 2.0 shouted, "what kind of new trouble is this?"

"The ship must have hit something underwater," said Newton. "A rock, maybe?"

"There are no rocks in the bay," said Silver Shield, and the worried look returned to his face. "After all, this is a port. I'm afraid that . . ."

Now the ship split in two, and one part of it sank into the depths of the sea. The other half remained burning on the surface. Another explosion was heard, and the second half of the ship smashed to pieces that scattered over the water and sank, one after the other. The group continued watching the water in horror. Now they could see numerous bubbles and swift, powerful whirlpools where the ship had sunk.

"What's going on over there?" asked Newton.

"Just what we were afraid of," said Silver Shield with a soldier's calm and composure. He pulled out his large sword with one hand, and with the other one took the silver shield off his back. "Something infiltrated the bay waters while the Firewall wasn't working."

"Something?" asked Super Media 2.0. "What?"

"Something ..." said Silver Shield quietly, "something that shouldn't have entered."

Chapter 5

Silver Shield walked down towards the beach, holding his sword in one hand and the silver shield in the other, and surveyed the water. The other three looked at him from their place of safety on the hill. The water had settled down and now looked completely tranquil.

"Look at that," Zuto whispered. Another whirlpool of bubbles disturbed the water again close to the shore, and from it emerged a huge black and writhing worm (see Zutopedia) with yellow rings adorning its body and gleaming scales. The worm slithered quickly out of the water and over the ground, heading towards the center of the world.

Silver Shield started chasing it. When the worm felt the approaching threat, it stopped, raised its head, and turned towards him. Silver Shield stood to confront it, his sword and shield ready. The worm raised itself higher and higher, until it towered over the anti-virus, and opened a mouth wreathed with two hundred and fifty-six long teeth.

Zuto, Newton, and Super Media 2.0 held their breath. Suddenly, the worm shot its head forward and spit a flame of fire at Silver Shield. He quickly hid behind his shield, which absorbed most of the fire and started heating up.

Now it was his turn to attack. He ran towards the worm in an attempt to strike it with his sword. The worm swerved, evading the sword, and just as quickly lifted its tail and struck the anti-virus forcefully. Silver Shield was flung some distance away and landed on the ground. Before he had time to recover from the blow, the worm crawled on top of him with its heavy body and once again spat fire at his face. At the last moment, poor Silver Shield managed to raise his shield and block the flames with it, but this time, the shield became so hot that he was forced to throw it away. Sensing an approaching victory, the worm lifted its head and took a deep breath in order to land a fatal blow. Silver Shield's body was trapped under its weight, and he covered his face with his hands helplessly.

Suddenly, something smashed into the worm and it rolled aside, emitting a surprised squeak. It was Zuto, who jumped on the worm and grabbed its throat while it rolled and twisted on the ground. But the worm was not yet beaten. It started coiling its body around Zuto, crushing him. Slippery Zuto managed to escape its stranglehold and rolled on the ground next to it, panting heavily.

Silver Shield recovered, charged the worm, hit it with his sword with all of his might, and beheaded it with one stroke. The black corpse quickly crumbled, and after a short while all that remained was a pile of two hundred and fifty-six teeth.

Super Media 2.0 and Newton ran towards them.

"Are you okay?" asked Super Media 2.0.

"Yes," Zuto answered, still panting. He brushed off the grass and dirt that had stuck to him when he rolled on the ground.

"You just did a good deed," said Silver Shield.

"Uh, yes," said Zuto in embarrassment. "It was nothing."

Silver Shield offered his hand and Zuto took it.

"Wait a moment," said Super Media 2.0 and took several steps backward. "I want to take a picture of this his-his-historical handshake."

Zuto and Silver Shield looked at her in wonder as they shook hands. She blinked and a *ssss . . . click* sound was heard. "That's it. Got it."

"Hey!" said Zuto, "I didn't know that you can take pictures."

"Didn't you notice me doing that?" she said and laughed. "I-I've already taken several pic-pictures since we met. Here, look."

Light beamed from her eyes, and a clear picture of Zuto sitting on the motorcycle in the Recycle Bin appeared several steps ahead of her. The group gathered around Super Media 2.0 and smiled as they looked at the pictures she projected.

A strange noise interrupted them once more, coming from the direction of the bay. A mass of bubbles rose to the water's surface, and little whirlpools started eddying near the shore.

"I'm such a fool," said Silver Shield. "Another worm is hiding in the water!"

Before even the anti-virus managed to complete his sentence, the second worm leapt out of the water. However, this one had learned from its predecessor's unfortunate experience, and emerged onto the shore far away from them. It nimbly climbed over the cables that led bits from the port's warehouse towards the world's inner cities, and started slithering along them swiftly. In a blink of an eye it disappeared over the horizon.

Wordlessly, the anti-virus ran across the hill, gathering his shield on the way. He mounted his bike and started chasing the worm.

"Let's follow him," Zuto called. "He may need our help again."

Zuto, Super Media 2.0, and Newton ran along the cables and were soon deep inland, far away from the port. The cables led them to a desert-like area, arid and hot, where they finally met up again with Silver Shield, confused and frustrated.

"This is what's become of the worm," he said and pointed at a big, black cocoon of scales, its diameter twice the size of his height, connected to the ground by hundreds of sticky threads.

"I arrived just as it finished building this cocoon around itself with a substance it had secreted from its mouth," he explained. "But by the time I came closer, it had already finished. My sword can't penetrate this shell of scales, nor can it tear the threads." He demonstrated this by striking the cocoon and the threads that fastened it to the ground. They heard muffled thuds, but the cocoon was neither cracked nor dented, and the thick, sticky, mesh of threads was intact.

"I don't know what this is," he concluded, embarrassed.

Newton placed the little wooden box that served as his speaker's platform on the ground and stood on it. "Methinks," he said, "that this is some sort of stage in the life of the worm. Within some unknown period of time, a new creature will emerge from this cocoon." He closed his eyes for a minute and thought. "Maybe even more than one," he added.

Zuto approached the cocoon and kicked it. "Owwww," he shouted and held his foot while jumping up and down on the other one. The cocoon didn't even tremble.

"Extremely disturbing," said Silver Shield. "I will have to return to headquarters and search my books.

Perhaps I'll find a description of this ... this thing, though I doubt it."

"What will you do if you don't find a description?" asked Super Media 2.0, worried.

"I shall be forced to issue a message to the user that a worm of an unidentified type has infiltrated the computer, and that I cannot remove it." Silver Shield stared at the ground and looked tired and miserable. "This is a grave turn of events," he mumbled.

Now wailing sirens were piercing the air. Shortly after, four yellow squad cars belonging to the Operating System appeared on site. About twenty agents exited them, wearing yellow coats with the words "Operating System" on their backs. They started wandering around the area, writing down comments in their notebooks and scratching their heads.

"You should go now," whispered Silver Shield to Zuto and his friends, "otherwise I'll have a hard time trying to explain what a virus and two software applications who are supposed to be in the Recycle Bin are doing here. If you walk away quietly, maybe they won't notice you."

"Perhaps these agents can help you get rid of the worm?" whispered back Super Media 2.0.

"No"—Silver Shield laughed bitterly—"they just came to assess the damage."

"What a shame," Super Media 2.0 said in disappointment.

"It's not your problem," Silver Shield said, trying to console her. "At worst they'll install a better anti-virus to take my place. . . . Now go . . ."

Chapter 6

Right next to the Recycle Bin, there was a cable that didn't lead anywhere. It drained unnecessary bits from all over the world. The bits glided on the cable until they reached its exposed edge, where they fell on the ground and melted. This created a little bluish lake, which was Zuto and Newton's favorite hangout place.

The two were floating on two large rubber tubes that they found in the Recycle Bin, and Super Media 2.0 stood on the muddy shore and looked at them worriedly. The tube that they brought for her floated uselessly in the water.

"Come on, Super Media 2.0," called Zuto. "Stop being such a scaredy-cat . . . the water's nice."

Super Media 2.0 hesitated. "Wait a moment," she answered. "First, I'll take your picture."

"Okay," said Zuto. "Now get in!"

She walked into the water, her steps slow and graceful. When the water reached her hair ribbons, she dove in, and then emerged wet and swam towards her tube. "This really is fun," she admitted. She lay back on her tube and closed her eyes.

"Do you think," she asked after they had floated on the water for some time, "that the cocoon is dangerous?"

"No," said Zuto. "You heard Silver Shield's explanation. If he fails dealing with that pest, another anti-virus will be installed to take care of it. We have no cause for worry."

Super Media 2.0 considered that. "Although I feel bad for Silver Shield," she said, "I can't wait for the cocoon to be re-removed and eliminated already. Even if a better anti-virus arrives, he might fail too. And what will happen then?"

"They'll format the computer," interjected Newton, lying peacefully on his tube with his eyes closed.

"What?" asked Super Media 2.0. "What does that mean?"

Newton sat up and opened his eyes. "It means," he said, "complete obliteration of the entire world. Everything we know will be destroyed: the cocoon, the ports, me, you . . . Zuto . . . everything."

"But that's just dreadful!" Super Media 2.0 cried and sat up in her tube. "Why-w-w-w-why, w-why would anyone do something like that? Who would do something like that?"

"The user," said Newton. "If he receives a message that there's a worm that can't be eliminated in his computer, he'll have no choice. He'll erase everything and start from scratch. Otherwise, the worm will ruin everything anyway and also infiltrate other computers."

"Maybe we sh-should do something about it?"

"Like what?" asked Zuto.

"I don't know. . . ." Super Media 2.0 thought for a minute. "Maybe we should join forces with Silver Shield a-a-and together eliminate the worm."

"You've watched too many movies, my dear," Newton chuckled.

"Of course," she smiled, "I'm a media player. But still . . . I think it's a mistake to do nothing more than f-float here on the water, having fun, while there's this threat hovering over the very existence of our world. What d-do you think?"

Zuto and Newton continued lying on their rubber tubes and didn't answer.

"Why, Zuto already h-helped eliminate one of the worms," she continued. "Wouldn't you like to finish the job?"

"I tried kicking the cocoon," replied Zuto, "and I almost broke my foot. I don't know what else we can do."

"There's something you don't understand, Super Media 2.0," said Newton.

"What?" she asked.

"We're all in the Recycle Bin now," he answered lightheartedly and crossed his arms under his head. "The world dumped us here because we're worthless. We're less than worthless. Losers like us can't do anything useful."

Super Media 2.0 was shocked at having the painful truth flung in her face so unexpectedly. "We're not n-no-nothing," she tried to protest. "We're not n-n-n-" she gave up and lapsed into quiet, sad thoughts.

"Virus attack!" Zuto shouted suddenly. He jumped on Super Media 2.0's rubber tube and capsized it.

Super Media 2.0 emerged from the water laughing. She caught Zuto, who still held on to her tube, and threw him into the water. Zuto dived and surfaced, giggling, under Newton's tube, capsizing it as well.

"Wha-what?" Newton managed to sputter before he fell into the water.

The three friends played, fooled around, and rested in the water for a very long time. The worm, the cocoon, the anti-virus, the danger to their world, all were forgotten for a while.

"Are you of the same opinion as Newton," asked Super Media 2.0 later on, "that we're w-w-worthless?"

She and Zuto were still floating on the lake, while Newton slept on his rubber tube on the other side.

"Uhhhh," Zuto hesitated, "yeah."

"That's why you stole the motorbike," said Super Media 2.0, "just like you explained before. To feel i-i-important."

"Yes," admitted Zuto.

"But that's not true, that you're worthless," she protested. "You and Newton, both of you are very special. Why, Newton in-invented this theory. He has to be the smartest software in th-the entire world. And you too . . . you're brave and agile."

Zuto blushed.

"Why, your ability to sq-squeeze out of any situation, difficult as it may be, is extraordinary. You managed to steal Silver Shield's bi-bike and perform that stunt with the Firewall. Then you escaped Silver Shield again, and then fought the worm—I think that you're the quickest, craf . . . tiest, bravest creature I've ever met in my life. You just have to cha-channel your efforts into good deeds, just like you did with the battle against the worm near the port."

"Maybe," said Zuto and closed his eyes, carried away by daydreams. "Maybe if I accomplished several more brave and useful deeds, I would become a really important creature!"

"If you want it badly e-enough, then it will eventually happen. That's how it is in the movies."

Zuto smiled.

Suddenly, Super Media 2.0 started playing music. She played an old, gentle, soothing melody she was very fond of. As usual, the notes got stuck occasionally, and Zuto filled the pauses with soft, improvised whistles that somehow fit right in and created a harmonious symphony.

"That was lovely together," said Super Media 2.0 when she finished playing.

"Yes," said Zuto. Silence descended. He looked at her and she smiled at him, her hair ribbons long and shiny. All of a sudden he realized that he liked her a lot.

"I like being here with you," she said and closed her eyes.

Suddenly, an unfamiliar buzz disrupted the calm.

"What's that?" Super Media 2.0 opened her eyes in alarm.

"I don't know," Zuto answered.

"Newton," called Super Media 2.0, "wake up! Something's happening."

Newton woke up on the other side of the lake, blinking his eyes.

"Do you recognize that buzz?"

"No," said Newton, stretching and yawning, "but I think I can guess what it is."

"Well, what?" asked Super Media 2.0.

"I think that . . ." Newton sat up on his tube and searched the sky with his eyes. "There it is . . . over there." He pointed at a little gold plane high in the sky.

"It's flying straight at us," said Super Media 2.0.

"Yes, yes," said Newton. "It's a new anti-virus. It's probably here for—"

"Run, Zuto!" yelled Super Media 2.0, "it's chasing you!"

She hadn't finished speaking when the plane shot an arrow at Zuto. The arrow hit the rubber tube, and a noisy stream of air started pouring out, propelling Zuto towards the center of the lake. Zuto jumped into the water and disappeared. The plane dove and then flew low over the lake, searching for him. It was a small propeller plane with a pair of wings at the front and a smaller pair at the back, all painted gold.

Super Media 2.0 and Newton jumped off their tubes and started swimming out of the lake. The plane flew low over them, raising a huge wave of water that almost drowned them. The plane continued its search and started circling the lake, leaving them struggling in the stormy waters.

Super Media 2.0 held on to Newton and together they overcame the waves and crawled, exhausted, to the shore.

"I hope Zuto isn't hurt," she said, staring worriedly at the stormy lake. There was no sign of the greenish virus. The plane soared and then dove again, shooting another volley of arrows.

"Can he hold his breath underwater for so long?" wondered Super Media 2.0.

The plane continued flying high in the sky, diving every now and again to attack some suspicious target. It kept on doing this for a long while, but still Zuto was nowhere to be found.

Newton leaned towards Super Media 2.0. "Look over there," he whispered, "but carefully! Don't turn your head."

Super Media 2.0 looked cautiously out of the corner of her eyes in the direction that Newton had pointed out to her, keeping her head straight forward. She saw the tip of the cable from which the bits poured into the lake, and Zuto climbing slowly and quietly up the pole that supported it.

"Oh!" Super Media 2.0 whispered, filled with joy. "Good for Zuto. The plane doesn't see him. . . . It's searching for him in the water."

The plane continued flying over the lake, scanning the water, while Zuto climbed up the pole slowly and silently. When he reached the edge of the cable, he scrambled up and stood on it. He waved to them and turned to sneak away, slouching stealthily. But then he slipped and fell on the cable, his legs splayed, and by mistake, kicked one of the bits that had just passed beneath him. The bit fell, hit the pole with a loud clanging noise, and fell into the water. The plane turned sharply and started flying towards him.

"He's been detected," called Newton.

"You've been discovered, Zuto," shouted Super Media 2.0. "Run!"

Zuto shot to his feet and started running away on the cable while arrows whistled around him. The plane chased him, and the two disappeared over the horizon.

"It seems as though this anti-vi-vi-virus is more of a threat to Zuto than Silver Shield was," mumbled Super Media 2.0. "P-poor Zuto. Will we be able to help him?"

"We have to return to the Recycle Bin," replied Newton. "I think we'll meet someone there whom we can consult."

Chapter 7

You may have forgotten by now, but our story takes place in one boy's computer, Tom is his name, and the time now is six minutes and thirteen seconds past three, meaning that forty-six seconds have passed since the story began. Just a short while ago, at five minutes and thirty-nine seconds past three, twelve seconds after the beginning of the story, a message appeared on Tom's screen reading: "An unidentified worm has been discovered. The anti-virus cannot remove it." That was when Zuto and his friends arrived at the lake and started playing there.

Luckily, there was a disk with a new anti-virus program on Tom's desk: Golden Fortress. His dad had bought it several days earlier, and Tom hadn't had the time to install it yet. Now is a great time to do that, Tom thought. He inserted the disk into the drive and quickly installed the new anti-virus. And so, at six minutes and thirteen seconds past three, the new anti-virus started working, and our friends saw the results of its efforts in the lake, as we have just described.

Now, only fourteen seconds remain until the end of the story, but as we've already mentioned, many things happen inside a computer in the course of a second, and indeed, the better part of our story still lies ahead of us.

Super Media 2.0 and Newton returned to the field that was at the heart of the Recycle Bin. Silver Shield sat there on the box, his hands covering his face. His motorcycle lay on its side behind him.

"Just as I expected," said Newton. "Here he is, the deposed anti-virus."

Silver Shield lifted his head and gazed at them.

"Yes, I've been thrown into the Recycle Bin," he said, "and rightfully so, I might add. After all, I have failed at my assignment."

"And the cocoon?" Super Media 2.0 demanded, "what ha-happens with the cocoon now?"

"It's still there, where I left it," Silver Shield answered and lowered his gaze again. "I'm such a failure . . . I'm ashamed of myself."

"Stop it," said Super Media 2.0. "You're not a failure. After all, you protected our world su-successfully for such a long time, and everyone owes you a big tha-thank you. It's only natural that there comes a time when you ha-have to retire and make way for a ne-newer anti-virus."

"Yes," answered Silver Shield, slightly encouraged. "Let's hope at least that Golden Fortress, the new anti-virus, will know how to handle that cocoon."

"In the meantime he's busy chasing Zuto," said Super Media 2.0.

"Really?" Silver Shield said in surprise. "Did you see him?"

Super Media 2.0 closed her eyes briefly, and when she opened them again, a light shone from them. She projected one of the pictures she had taken earlier, in which the golden plane was flying over the lake.

"Hmmm," said Silver Shield. "That's just one of Golden Fortress' planes. He has an army of planes, and tanks as well. He controls them all from his fortress."

"Which means that Zuto is in serious trouble," Super Media 2.0 said in concern. "I told you that it was a mistake to sit around doing nothing while the co-cocoon wasn't yet eliminated. And while we were having fun at the l-lake, the situation deteriorated."

Just then, Zuto appeared in the middle of the field, all dirty and bruised.

"Zuto!" called Super Media 2.0. She ran towards him, and he collapsed into her arms.

"Oh, no!" she cried. A large golden arrow had pierced the green virus's shoulder from the back, and he looked as if he was about to faint. She carried him and carefully placed him on the little box that Silver Shield had vacated.

"Ooh . . . ummm . . . hmmm . . ." Zuto mumbled incoherently.

Silver Shield stepped closer to examine him. The arrow was stuck very deep, and its sharp tip protruded from the front of his shoulder.

"It isn't a serious injury," said the seasoned anti-virus. "I've seen viruses of your kind recover from graver injuries. All we have to do is pull out the arrow."

He broke the arrow's sharp tip. "This is going to hurt terribly," he said, "but just for a little while." He clasped the shaft of the arrow forcefully and pulled it back. Zuto screamed.

"Are you all right now, Zuto?" Super Media 2.0 asked with concern.

Zuto sat up and rubbed his throbbing shoulder. "Better," he answered weakly. "They almost killed me," he added. "The first plane was joined by three more, and the four of them showered arrows on me. I barely managed to avoid them and ran as fast as I could towards a city I saw in the horizon, where I thought I could disappear from sight. One of the arrows hit me at the entrance to the city."

He paused and rubbed his shoulder again.

"I ran on a cable that led into one of the houses, and crept in through the window. There was a table there, covered with a yellow tablecloth, and several workers stood around it and sorted a heap of bits piled on it. When they saw me they panicked and started fleeing down the stairs. I overturned the table and everything on it scattered on the floor. Then I threw it out the window to confuse the planes. I heard them shooting hordes of arrows at it. Then, I lifted the yellow tablecloth, draped it over myself, ran down the stairs with the workers, and got out of the house. The planes were looking for something green—he smiled painfully—"not yellow, and that's how I managed to escape the city. With the little strength I had left, I came back here." (In fact, the workers that Zuto ran into were busy with a task related to playing a song that Tom instructed his new media player, Super Media 3.0, to play. The incident caused a rude disruption in the music, and Tom started wondering if the new version stuttered as well.)

"Well done, Zuto," Super Media 2.0 said and hugged him. "That was a chase just like in the movies."

"But those planes were too quick for me," said Zuto. "It was scary. . . ."

"Golden Fortress will probably be furious," said Silver Shield, "now that you've slipped through his fingers. Those planes you saw are but a fraction of his army, and he'll turn all his forces against you now. You'll have to hide here and not show your nose, not even for a tiny moment."

Zuto looked extremely miserable and lost in thought. "Hide?" he said. "Just when I thought that I can start doing important and worthy deeds, I have to go into hiding because of some grouchy anti-virus?" He rose from the box and started pacing. "Anyway," he added, "he'll find me sooner or later, and then what?"

"You don't have a choice," said Super Media 2.0 gently. "Golden Fortress' planes are se-sear-searching for you out there. They'll kill you if you don't hide."

"So I'll have to run away from here," said Zuto desperately.

"Where will you go?" asked Silver Shield.

"I'll run away to . . . I'll run away . . . ." Zuto searched his memory but to no avail. He fell silent and seemed lost in thought again. Suddenly, he had an idea and he jumped up and stood on the box. "I'll run away to the sea!" he declared enthusiastically. "I'll sneak on one of the ships and sail with it! It'll bring me to another world, and if I don't like it . . . I'll run away again! I'll live at sea . . . maybe even get my own ship . . ." He gazed at his friends.

"It'll be so sad if you leave," said Super Media 2.0.

Silver Shield and Newton nodded.

Super Media 2.0's words touched Zuto's heart. He didn't really want to leave his friends and the Recycle Bin and the lake and all the places he loved. His sudden enthusiasm faded away just as quickly as it came.

"Also, it's not as simple as you describe it," said Silver Shield. "If you do board a ship, I'm not sure that the Firewall will let you pass. Sometimes it identifies stowaways and burns down the entire ship. You'll have to jump over it again, but this time without my bike."

"And sailing the seas isn't a simple matter," added Newton. "Many dangers lurk at sea, and some ships are lost there."

Silence descended. Super Media 2.0 wiped off the last traces of dirt on Zuto's face with her hands.

"Actually, you do have another option," said Silver Shield suddenly. "There's something that I haven't told you yet."

The three friends looked at him in surprise.

"What?" asked Zuto.

"A secret from the past," said Silver Shield. "From *your* past, Zuto. I think it's about time that you found out about it."

Chapter 8

Silver Shield sat down on the box, and the rest of the group sat on the ground around him. He started his story: "It happened many and many a clock cycle ago. I was a young, vigorous anti-virus. My motorcycle was shiny and polished, the latest model at the time, and I wandered proudly around the world. And then, during one routine patrol, I met a virus. I recognized him immediately: Zutrog-33."

"That's me!" Zuto declared proudly.

"No," said the anti-virus. "I haven't gotten to you yet in the story. I had never come across a virus of this kind until then, but I was well trained for this encounter. He looked like Zuto, but he had a foolish expression and an evil smile."

"That certainly isn't me!" said Zuto. "But how did he enter the computer? Did he jump over the Firewall?"

"No. The Firewall only guards the ports. Don't forget that there are many entrances into our world. He entered through one of the disk drives, piggybacking on some software, whose name I can't remember. Anyway, when I saw him, I pulled out my sword, and we fought. He tried to defend himself, but I was too strong for him and I destroyed him. I knew that such a virus duplicates himself, and that by now, there must be many copies of him in the computer, so I embarked on a quest to hunt them down. I found their kind in many places I visited, and destroyed them one by one. . . ." Silver Shield sighed yearningly. "Those were the days," he said. He looked at Zuto sadly and continued his story. "After a while, I destroyed them all, and peace and quiet were restored to the world, or so I thought. But then, after I had forgotten all about it, I was surprised to see another one; similar, yet different from the viruses I had destroyed."

"Me!" Zuto declared proudly.

"No," said Silver Shield, "not yet . . . it was your father."

Zuto was surprised and amazed. He continued listening with growing attention.

"He had deep, wise eyes, and he looked at me quietly. I tried to strike him, but he managed to escape. I never saw anyone run as fast as he did; he was even faster than you, Zuto. He leapt off the ground and landed on the roof of one of the houses. It was one incredible leap, and then he disappeared. I searched for him for a long time, until eventually, I ran into him in one of the alleys. I stormed him with a drawn sword, but this time, instead of running away, he held his ground and shot me!"

"Did he have a weapon?" asked Zuto, fascinated.

"No!" said the anti-virus. "He simply moved his hands and then shot blue lightning from them, just like magic. The lightning hit my shield and almost smashed it. I realized then he was a mutation: he was one of the clones of the original Zutrog-33, but something in his duplication 'went wrong,' and had turned him into a much more sophisticated, powerful virus.

"Afterwards, I continued chasing him, but much more carefully. I was afraid of him. I tried to follow him and learn his ways. He was different from a regular virus. He didn't try to duplicate himself, and didn't try to do any harm whatsoever. I couldn't understand him. Finally, I managed to ambush him and surprise him. I struck his leg with my sword and managed to amputate it. He turned towards me and did those magical movements again, and the blue lightning hit me with great force and threw me back. I lay on the floor, too scared to get up. From my place on the floor, I saw him move his hands strangely. This time, they emitted green smoke that assumed a shape, and all of a sudden another virus was created. He had created a copy of himself."

"Me?" asked Zuto.

"Yes," Silver Shield continued. "It was you. 'Run,' he said to you and you fled. After that, he sat down, pressed his palms together, and fell into some kind of a coma. I watched him for a long time until I mustered my courage to get up, approach him, and examine him. He didn't move a muscle. And that's the end of the story."

"Wow," said Zuto. "That's an amazing story. Are you saying that I too can shoot lightning from my hands?" He flailed his arms about, but nothing happened.

"You have to meet your father again," said Silver Shield. "He can probably teach you to jump and run like him. Maybe to do magic like him too. If he does, it'll be easier for you to deal with Golden Fortress, and you won't have to hide or escape to another world."

"That'll be marvelous!" Super Media 2.0 cried enthusiastically. "You'll be ju-j-ju-j-just like the superheroes in the movies!"

Zuto clapped excitedly. "Finally I'll be . . . someone!"

"You mean to say that Zuto's father is still around?" Newton wondered. "Didn't you destroy him after he fell into a coma?"

"No," said Silver Shield, "I was smarter than that. Since I'd never come across such a phenomenon before, I ordered that we store him in the Hard Drive. As far as I know, he's still there."

"The Hard Drive can maintain information for a very long time," said Newton. "It's its job. If you didn't order the virus's deletion, he's probably still there."

Silver Shield stood up, went to his motorcycle, and poked around in the small trunk.

"Here it is," he called finally, pulling out a piece of paper with a scribble on it and handing it over to Zuto.

"What's that?" the virus asked.

"These are instructions on how to find your father in the Hard Drive."

Zuto tried to turn the page this way and that, confused. "I don't understand what's written here," he said.

"You're not supposed to understand," the anti-virus answered. "You have to go with that piece of paper to the Disk Controller. That's where they handle requests to take something in or out of the Hard Drive. They'll know what to do."

"Aren't you joining us?" asked Zuto.

The silver robot had already gotten on his bike.

"No," answered Silver Shield. "I'm going to visit Golden Fortress. I want to have a word with him. I think he should leave you alone for now and focus on the mysterious cocoon." He started his bike and activated the siren and the flickering blue light.

"Good luck!" he said loudly and drove away.

Chapter 9

The Disk Controller was a calm, pleasant corner of the world, far away from the Recycle Bin. A path of red bricks led there, winding through green fields, ending at a courtyard paved with red bricks as well. A gleaming black fence crossed the fields from one side of the horizon to the other, and beyond it, the hills of the Hard Drive (see Zutopedia) towered, covered with endless rows of white stone bits.

Actually, the Disk Controller was no more than a little shack, loaded with gadgets and stacks of paper folders. The three friends walked down the path until they reached the courtyard, and looked at the shack.

Complete silence prevailed. Even the wind that usually blew there had abated.

"The Controller looks abandoned," said Zuto, looking at the empty shack.

"I'm not sure," Newton answered as he approached the shack. "The lazy workers are probably asleep."

Newton walked towards the large reception window at the front of the shack.

"Hey!" he called. "Is anybody here?"

Silence.

"Perhaps there's a bell?" suggested Super Media 2.0, and Newton started searching.

"That's odd," said Zuto.

Suddenly, a creature's head peeked out of the window. He resembled the Operating System agents whom they had come across earlier. Unlike them, he wore a blue overall. He was the driver of the Disk Controller.

"Yes, buddies," he said. "What're you doing here and how can I help you?"

Before any of them had time to answer, the driver yawned widely, rubbed his eyes, and straightened his clothes. It seemed as though he really did just wake up from a nap.

"We have to take something out of the Hard Drive," said Newton confidently.

"Buddy," declared the driver, "you've come to the right place. Do you have a file name?" He scrutinized the threesome in interest. "Isn't that a . . . virus?" he asked in amazement when his eyes fell on Zuto.

"Uh . . . not exactly . . ." Newton was at a loss for words. "That's Zuto. He . . . he's actually a kind of . . . kind of . . ." he searched his mind in an attempt to find a reasonable explanation concerning Zuto's nature. "He's a virus," he finally said after failing to find one. Zuto bowed.

The driver stared at them silently. "Whatever, buddy," he said finally. "It doesn't matter to me. Do you have a file name?"

"Yes," Newton said and handed him the paper.

The driver examined it. "virus_sample492.bin" was written on it.

"Let me check," he said and went to the cabinet behind him. He returned to the window with a pile of folders, put them on his desk, and started leafing through them while humming an old song to himself.

"I found it; here it is," he said and pointed to a page in the open folder before him. "Sector 2F3B," he continued and emerged from the shack. "It's not far from here. Do you want to come with me?"

"Can we?" Zuto asked in surprise.

"Of course, green buddy," replied the driver. "After all, you don't want me to get bored driving the entire way all by myself." He started crossing the red courtyard towards the fence. "Come on, follow me," he said.

He led them to a gate in the fence. Newton turned an inquisitive eye towards the gate as they passed through; various appliances surrounded it. Beyond the gate sprawled the endless grassy hills of the Hard Drive. Sixteen tractors stood in line nearby, a small wagon hitched to the rear of each one.

"Why do you need so many tractors?" wondered Zuto.

"When things get busy, I employ other workers to help me," the driver explained. He climbed one of the tractors and tried to sit in the driver's seat, but Zuto ran and beat him to it.

"Will you let me drive?" he asked.

"No, buddy," the driver answered. "That's my job."

Newton and Super Media 2.0 climbed up and sat on the tractor behind the driver. Zuto joined them, disappointed. The driver started the engine, and they began driving through the green hills.

Silver Shield turned the accelerator grip of the motorcycle as far as it could go. He knew that the cocoon was a time bomb that was going to explode at any moment, and he was concerned that Golden Fortress wasn't treating the matter seriously enough. He rode towards his old headquarters: a small, rectangular structure, full of equipment, with a tall antenna on its roof. When he arrived there, his jaw dropped in astonishment. A huge fortress now towered where his old headquarters had been, surrounded by golden walls. One thousand and twenty-four golden turrets of various heights rose between the walls, with flags fluttering proudly on their spires. Golden tanks toured the periphery, and dozens of golden planes buzzed above, landing and taking off using circular landing fields built on the turrets.

Silver Shield's heart filled with envy. If only I had these forces at my disposal, he thought. He approached the fortress' gate and pressed the buzzer installed next to it. From within the wall a robotic eye stationed on a telescoping arm emerged and glared at him.

"Yes?" said the eye in a metallic voice.

"Uhhh," said Silver Shield, "I came to meet Golden Fortress."

"And you are . . . ?" asked the eye.

"I'm . . ." Silver Shield wondered how to introduce himself. "I'm . . . I'm . . . his predecessor. I have information for him. Important information."

"Do you?" said the eye. It retreated into the wall and disappeared.

After several clock cycles, the gate opened. Silver Shield walked into a hall made of fancy white stone.

"Follow the arrows!" called a metallic voice that echoed in the spacious hall. Lamps set in the floor created shimmering arrows that led him towards the elevator. The elevator doors closed behind him, and a green stripe of light immediately appeared and scanned his body from head to toe.

"Clean!" the voice announced, and the elevator started moving.

When the elevator came to a halt, its doors opened into a large, lavish hall. Gigantic columns of marble ran along both sides of the hall, and among them stood statues depicting heroes fighting mythical monsters. At the end of the hall stood an elevated wooden podium. Four stairs covered by a red carpet led to it. On the podium rested a huge golden head. Numerous thin wires, connected to the wall behind it, emerged from its metallic scalp instead of hair. This was Golden Fortress.

"So what are we actually looking for?" asked the driver of the Disk Controller after driving quite a distance.

"Ummm . . ." said Zuto, "We're bringing back my . . . um . . . my father."

"Oh," the driver said excitedly, "a family reunion! What an honor this is for me!"

"When will we get there?" asked Zuto, who was growing a bit impatient. "Are we close?"

"Yep, buddy, we're already at sector 2030," answered the driver, and only then did Zuto notice that the sector numbers were indicated by little signs scattered along the path on which they drove. "Another F0B sectors and we're there," the driver added.

"F0B?" Zuto asked, confused.

"Ah," the driver laughed. "We're used to talking in hexadecimal numbers" (see Zutopedia). "It's the usual counting method here. Three thousand, eight hundred, and fifty-one for you, buddy. Another three thousand, eight hundred, fifty-one sectors and we're there."

"Maybe you've changed your mind about letting me drive?" Zuto tried again. "Just for a short while."

"Hmmm . . ." the driver thought for a moment. "Well . . . actually, why not."

The driver stopped the tractor, swapped places with Zuto, and showed him how to drive the large vehicle. Zuto approached the task enthusiastically.

"Oh, Zuto," said Super Media 2.0 who almost slid off the seat that she shared with Newton, "we have to fo-focus on the assignment at hand and not fool around. I'm afraid something will happen."

"But you're always afraid of something," said Zuto, wearing a huge grin. He passed by sector 2030 without any mishap and gradually gathered speed. His grin widened even more. Sector 2031 passed by as well, and at sector 2032 the tractor was almost flying.

"Not so fast," the driver of the Disk Controller tried to warn him, but it was too late. The left wheel hit a rock, the tractor bounced, and its passengers almost fell off. Zuto turned the steering wheel sharply and they strayed off the path into sector 2033, leaving behind a trail of scattered bit-stones, until the tractor stalled deep in the heart of the sector.

Newton chuckled. "That was fun," he said. "Like a ride in an amusement park."

"I told you so," Super Media 2.0 scolded him.

"I'm sorry," said Zuto with genuine remorse, examining the damage he left behind him.

"Um ... it's okay," the driver said. "I don't think there's anything important in this sector. Come on; help me gather the scattered bits."

He drove the tractor back to the path, and the group helped put the stones back and line them up in nice, tidy rows. (Actually, this sector contained a family photo that Tom once took. Of course, they didn't place the bits in the right order, and one of Tom's uncles now sported a colorful moustache.)

Chapter 10

"Do my eyes deceive me?" the large golden head said, his voice echoing in the hall, "or have I been 'honored' with a visit from my failing predecessor?" A thin, malevolent smile played on his thick lips.

"Yes . . ." Silver Shield answered and started crossing the hall towards the head. "You see—"

"And to what do I owe this dubious honor?" Golden Fortress interrupted him.

"I—" stammered the anti-virus awkwardly, "I—"

"Get to the point!" Golden Fortress' voice thundered in the large hall. "My time is short and there is much to be done."

"It's the worm," Silver Shield continued, trying to regain his focus while his metal feet knocked heavily against the marble floor. "It's extremely dangerous, I believe. Do you know what will emerge from that cocoon?"

"Not yet," admitted Golden Fortress. "The matter is under investigation."

"I have a feeling that we have to watch it carefully and prepare for the worst," said Silver Shield.

"Of course," Golden Fortress replied impatiently.

"And on the other hand," the silver robot continued, "we have Zuto . . . that is, Zutrog-33. I understand you ran into him."

"Yes," the gigantic head replied, "several of my planes almost eliminated him, but he escaped after sustaining injury." Anger flooded Golden Fortress as he remembered his first failure. He was ashamed that a little green virus, a mere Zutrog-33, could cause such difficulties to an innovative anti-virus such as himself. "I've allotted sixty-four out of my one hundred and twenty-eight planes for his final elimination," he added. "They're searching for him now. I believe that soon I will be able to announce the removal of the pest."

"That's what I've come to say," said Silver Shield, who had arrived at the end of the hall and now stood near the huge head. "Zuto isn't exactly a Zutrog-33. He's something of a mutation. He doesn't duplicate himself and doesn't cause much damage. I wanted to tell you that you should concentrate all your forces around the cocoon, and put them on the alert for when it will hatch. You can postpone the entire matter of Zuto for later on."

This only increased Golden Fortress' anger. "You, who failed in your duty, dare come to me and teach me priorities?" he yelled. "How long has he been wandering around our world, that green little creature whom you call 'Zuto'?" he added disparagingly.

"Ummm . . . that's not . . ." Silver Shield tried to reply, but once again lost his concentration in the face of the wrath of the gigantic head.

"You fell asleep while on duty, Silver Shield, and you were sloppy," Golden Fortress continued cruelly. "It's no wonder that as I take up my position as anti-virus I find a world in which one Zutrog-33 wanders about freely, and somewhere else a worm builds itself a cocoon. Now, allow me to deal with the mess you left behind by myself, as I see fit.

"This meeting is over," he added sharply. A blue velvet curtain emerged from both sides of the podium and surrounded it, concealing the head.

Silver Shield was upset by the criticism flung at him, but suddenly he felt his courage returning with a vengeance. He straightened up and announced in a clear, assertive voice, "I guarded the world for a long time and dealt successfully with many enemies. You, with all your modern equipment, haven't even served in your position for one thousand clock cycles, and yet, you've failed already. You'll have to work very hard to come up to the least of my achievements."

The blue curtain opened for a brief moment. "We'll see about that," said Golden Fortress, who peeked from behind it, and the curtain closed immediately.

"Yes, we will," said Silver Shield. He crossed his arms over his chest and turned to go.

"We've reached sector 2F39," announced the driver of the Disk Controller. "Over there," he added, pointing to the nearest hill, "that's sector 2F3A, and behind it is sector 2F3B, which is our destination."

Indeed, they soon reached a small sign reading "2F3B." It was a hill like any other hill, covered with green grass, and rows of white stones shaped as 0s or 1s were scattered densely upon it. The driver parked the tractor and climbed down.

"Come on," he said. "Now we have to collect the stones and place them on the wagon. It's important that we maintain the order of the stones and not confuse the bits with each other."

"Is my father buried under these stones?" asked Zuto, picking one up.

"No, buddy," the driver laughed. "Nothing is buried under these stones. The stones themselves—that's what we've come to collect."

"But there were stones just like these right by the gate," Zuto persisted. "Why did we drive all the way out here?"

"Well, it's not the stones themselves," the driver admitted. "It's the specific order of the bits here. That's why we've come here. They're encoding something. The bits on this hill are encoding your dad."

Zuto gave him a questioning look.

"Let's assume that there are viruses of two colors: green and black," the driver explained as he continued gathering bits and loading them on the wagon. "In order to encode the color of a virus, all you need is one bit. You just have to agree on an encoding table, for example zero for black and one for green."

"But there are many more colors, not just green and black."

"Exactly. Which is why we need more bits. Let's assume that there are four colors: black, green, blue, and red. We can encode them with the help of two bits: zero-zero for black, one-zero for green, zero-one for blue, and one-one for red," the driver explained.

"A blue virus?" Zuto laughed and tried to imagine that.

"With four bits you can encode sixteen different colors, and with eight bits you can encode two hundred and fifty-six colors. How many do you think you can encode with thirty-two bits?"

"Ummm," said Zuto, "one million?"

"Much more," replied the driver, "more than four billion."

"Four billion, two hundred and ninety-four million, nine hundred and sixty-seven thousand, two hundred and ninety six, to be precise," offered Newton, who up until now had been busy organizing the bits in the wagon as neatly as possible.

"Uh . . . yes," confirmed the driver.

"Wow," said Zuto, truly surprised.

"Just as you can encode colors, you can encode other characteristics: height, the size of the eyes and their color, the shape of the face, and much more. For example, you can save eight bits to encode body color, another five bits to encode the height, ten bits to encode the shape of the face, etc. In one sector, there's room for four thousand and ninety-six bits, so there's no need to scrimp. And you can store stuff in more than one sector. We have here a movie—I think it's called 'Tron'—that's saved on—now pay close attention—two million different sectors. It took me a long time to lay all the bits in place for that movie."

"Oh," said Super Media 2.0. "I know that movie. I once pla-pla-played it. At least, I tried."

They finished gathering all of sector 2F3B's four thousand and ninety-six bits, and now the stones lay tidily in the wagon. The driver turned the tractor around, and they started back towards the Controller.

"With this system, you can encode anything," the driver continued. "Movies, music, books, software. Anything. These stone bits can endure for a long time. Ages. If, say, someone turns off the computer, then all the blue bits gliding on the cables will disappear, as will we, and our entire world will black out. But these stone bits over here—they'll remain unchanged. That's why we save things here: so they will last."

After a long ride, this time without any mishaps, they returned to the Disk Controller. Next to the gate, attached to the fence, there was some kind of a machine with a big pipe protruding from it. The driver parked the tractor so that the wagon and the pile of bits on it were located right beneath the pipe. The group climbed down from the vehicle and followed the driver through the gate, to the other side of the fence.

"Here, everything's ready now," said the driver, entering his shack. "Look at the gate."

He started pressing all sorts of buttons on the machines in his shack and they started humming and clattering. Suddenly, the machine by the gate started rattling too, and the pipe sucked in all the bits in the wagon.

The group looked at the gate with intense anticipation.

A loud bang startled them, and sparks flew out of the machine. Then, more and more bangs and claps were heard, followed by flashes of light. Smoke and colorful sparks filled the gate and obscured it completely.

"That's it. I'm done," the driver said, leaving his shack and joining them.

The smoke started dispersing, and Zuto's father appeared before their eyes. He was old and wrinkly, but otherwise he looked just like Zuto. He sat on the grass in front of the gate, one leg folded beneath him and the other one missing. His palms were pressed against each other in front of his body and his eyes were closed.

"Yes," said Newton. "This is exactly how Silver Shield described him."

"Hmmm," said the driver, "I remember Silver Shield asking me to save this . . . creature. That was a long time ago. Right, I'll go take a nap in my shack now. Call me if you need anything else," and he disappeared inside his shack again.

"So, now what?" asked Newton.

Zuto looked at him uncomfortably.

"I think we should give Zuto and his father some time alone," said Super Media 2.0.

The three of them lifted the old, slumbering virus and gently carried him towards a nearby field, which was empty and hidden among the Hard Drive hills.

"This is a good p-place for you to talk. We'll leave you now," said Super Media 2.0. Newton joined her, and they started walking back towards the Recycle Bin.

Chapter 11

Zuto remained alone with his father in the green valley. He didn't really know what to do, so he paced around the sleeping figure and waited.

His father was still asleep.

Zuto clapped his hands and jumped up and down.

"Uh . . . Dad!" he called.

His father still didn't wake up.

"Hmmm," Zuto mumbled to himself and sat down in front of his father. Just like him, he folded his legs beneath him, pressed his palms together before his face, closed his eyes, and remained that way for a long time.

When he opened his eyes, he saw the old virus in the same position, but now his eyes were open, looking right back at him.

"What?" his father asked suddenly.

Zuto jerked in alarm. "What what?"

"What what what?" asked his father.

"What what what what?" asked Zuto, and then both of them lapsed into silence because they realized that this conversation wasn't going anywhere.

"Are you my father?" asked Zuto.

"I did create you, so you can call me that," answered the old-timer.

"A long time has passed since then," said Zuto. "You were kept in the Hard Drive all that time. We just took you out of there."

"Why?" asked the old virus.

"There's a new anti-virus in the world, Golden Fortress is his name, and he's very strong. He almost killed me, and now he's trying to finish the job. Silver Shield said you could help me deal with him."

"Ah, yes." Zuto's father laughed. "Silver Shield, I remember him. You say he was replaced by Golden Fortress? I hope it wasn't because of me."

"No," said Zuto, "there's some other issue with a worm that built a cocoon, and Silver Shield couldn't remove it."

"Hmmm," answered his father. "Tell me about it, please."

Zuto told him the whole story, from start to finish: about the motorcycle and the port, and about the Firewall that suddenly crashed, and the two worms that infiltrated the bay. And he went on to tell his father how he helped eliminate one of them, and how the second worm escaped and settled inside a cocoon.

"And what have you done since?" his father asked.

"Nothing," answered Zuto uncomfortably. "I played at the lake. With friends."

His father looked at him disappointedly.

"Should I have done something?" asked Zuto.

His father took a deep breath. "All my life, I hoped to do something important and worthy," he said. "I invested much time developing and honing my physical abilities, waiting for an opportunity. Silver Shield refused to understand that. He pursued me endlessly until finally, he chopped off my leg and my dreams. Now, you have this opportunity."

"We really are alike," said Zuto. "I also hope to do something important, but I'm not as strong as you are. I helped eliminate one worm, but I couldn't remove the cocoon. Now Golden Fortress is threatening to chop off my dream." Zuto gazed at his wrinkled father and added, "Silver Shield said that he had never seen any creature run as fast or jump as high as you had done. He said that you can also do magic. Shoot lightning. I'd really like to learn how to shoot lightning from my hands."

"Ahhh. Yes," said his father, "shooting lightning. Don't you know how to do that?"

"No," answered Zuto.

"Hmmm," answered his father. "Perhaps an error occurred during duplication."

Zuto was disappointed. "Maybe you can teach me?"

"I don't know how to teach something like that," said Zuto's father. "These are powers that you must discover on your own, within yourself. Try a few times. I'll watch you and then we'll see."

In the meantime, Silver Shield was speeding on his bike back to the Recycle Bin.

That foolish, arrogant Golden Fortress, he thought. He hasn't yet protected the world from any threat whatsoever and he's showing off already.

Just as these thoughts ran through his head, he remembered the cocoon and decided to pay it a private visit to see what was new over there. He turned the motorcycle towards his new destination and accelerated steadily. When he arrived, Silver Shield was horrified to discover that the cocoon was thirty-two times as big as its original size, with strong contractions rippling like waves over its shell, indicating that something was about to happen. Only three of Golden Fortress' planes hovered above, and one tank stood nearby. From the arrows and spears that littered the ground, Silver Shield could see that they had previously tried to shoot at the cocoon, but realized that its shell was resistant to their sharpest arrows and heaviest spears. The rest of the tremendous army was busy searching for Zuto.

Suddenly, an exceptionally strong contraction disturbed the cocoon.

Something is definitely going to happen now, Silver Shield thought and pulled out his sword.

Apparently, Golden Fortress thought so as well, because the three planes, controlled from his faraway fortress, flew low and approached it curiously.

Silver Shield raised his eyes. Now the cocoon was much higher than himself. The contractions that seized it had stopped, and it seemed as though something in it had died. He continued watching it alertly, but when nothing happened, he relaxed and returned his sword to the sheath hanging across his back. The planes also resumed their flight high above, bored.

Suddenly there was a loud noise and a powerful contraction rippled through the cocoon. A crack opened on top, and thick smoke started wafting out, covering the sky. Silver Shield tensed up again and drew his sword, ready for action. Two of the planes flew into the black cloud, lost their way, crashed into each other, and smashed into the ground in a red ball of fire.

Now a hole gaped at the bottom of the cocoon, and tiny worms started crawling out of it. It seemed as though Golden Fortress was confused and alarmed: the remaining plane and tank swayed from side to side like two drunks, trying unsuccessfully to regain their balance.

Silver Shield stared in shock. The tiny worms kept pouring out to the ground, and several of them crawled towards him. He trampled them with his feet.

Once again a large contraction shook the cocoon, tearing it to pieces. A huge black cloud billowed in its place. Several thousand worms poured onto the ground. Something moved within the cloud, and then Silver Shield heard what sounded like a deep sigh. The smoke started dispersing, and gradually revealed the creature that emerged from the cocoon. It was a black monster, as big as a mountain, with eight feet, four heads, and thick yellow rings circling its necks. It shook its heads from one side to the other, as if waking up from a deep sleep.

In his remote hall, Golden Fortress regained his senses. His plane and tank started shooting at the monster, and after a moment, six more planes appeared in the sky. Five new tanks lumbered up the hill, joining the attack on the monster. It flailed its heads wildly. Although the arrows and spears flung at the monster caused it considerable pain, they didn't penetrate the scaly armor that protected its body. It opened its four mouths and revealed red maws wreathed with five hundred and twelve teeth each, and a great roar shook the world. Then, it stormed the tanks furiously, trampling them effortlessly beneath its feet. Its four maws spit fire at the planes. They tried to evade the flames but the monster hunted them down, one by one. When it finished its work, it stretched its heads up high and emitted a great roar of victory. Then it turned and started marching on its eight legs towards the fortress of the new anti-virus.

The smoke wafting from the cocoon gathered into a thick, black cloud over the area and kept growing and spreading. Silver Shield, still shocked by what he saw, stood for a moment rooted in place. His thoughts galloped ahead.

Golden Fortress made a mistake, he thought. He should have concentrated all his forces here, for this crucial moment, just as I recommended. Now it's going to be difficult for him to regroup his army for a renewed attack, and this monster may destroy our world first.

Silver Shield jumped on his bike and turned it towards the Recycle Bin. "It's time to take matters into our own hands," he mumbled.

Chapter 12

"Maybe," said Zuto's father, "maybe I'll simply show you how it's done."

They were still sitting on the grass, not far from the Disk Controller. Zuto, who'd already tried every possible motion with his hands, was quite dejected. "Maybe you just don't know what you're capable of," his father added. "Maybe if you watched me you'd be able to imitate me."

"Maybe," Zuto agreed without much hope.

Zuto's father rose slowly to his one leg, and for a moment, perched on it without moving. Suddenly, he bent over and jumped so high that he disappeared.

"Wow!" Zuto exclaimed, and continued staring at the sky until his father landed back on the ground, rolled over, and then vaulted up and started hopping around the valley at an enormous speed. He completed ten rounds faster than Zuto could have done running on both legs. Then, he hopped back, stood next to Zuto, and flung his hands forward, towards one of the boulders scattered in the area. Blue lightning shot out of his hands, hit the boulder, and smashed it with a bang.

"Wow!" Zuto exclaimed again and applauded.

Zuto's father bowed slightly and smiled. "Now you," he said.

Zuto got up a little nervously, squeezed his eyes shut, and tried to channel all his power to his feet. After he thought that he had done that long enough, he jumped, but it was even lower than his usual jump. He broke into a sprint around the valley, but he didn't feel it was faster than usual. Finally, he returned, flung his hands forward towards one of the boulders, and . . . nothing happened.

"I failed," he said, lowering his eyes. "I'm nothing but an error in duplication."

He returned to his place and fell despondently on the grass. "Maybe I'll run away to sea after all. No one will notice my absence anyhow. And even if I drown there, it will be of no consequence."

A silence lingered.

"I've changed my mind," his father said suddenly. "I no longer think that an error in duplication has occurred."

"Why?" asked Zuto.

"I've watched you closely, and I see something in you. I see myself in you, just as I was in my youth. I still believe that you will discover your hidden powers eventually, and that they'll be greater even than my own. But for that, you need time."

He sat in the same position in which he had exited the Hard Drive and closed his eyes in concentration, as if preparing himself for something.

Zuto stood up and looked at him. "What are you doing?" he wondered.

"I'm leaving this world," the old-timer answered and opened his eyes again.

"What?!" Zuto was startled. "Just a moment . . . wait . . . why? But you can help eliminate the cocoon. This is the chance you've been waiting for."

Zuto's father sighed. "I'm old and tired," he replied. "And now that I've met you, I feel that I have accomplished my mission. I did something valuable in my life after all: I created you. And from now on, you will have to carry on our unique lineage by yourself." He closed his eyes again and suddenly, his body rising, he started hovering above the ground.

"No!" Zuto protested, running towards him, "don't leave! I'm not ready yet!" He clutched his father's leg and tried to pull him back down.

"Hey!" exclaimed his father. He opened his eyes, lost his focus, and fell back to the ground. He reorganized his limbs in his coma pose and looked at Zuto calmly and wisely. "You're ready," he said in a quiet voice. "You'll see."

His hushed words penetrated Zuto's heart, and he stopped resisting. The father closed his eyes and started levitating again. "Good-bye," he managed to whisper, just before evaporating into a greenish cloud.

"Zuto . . . Zuto!" Super Media 2.0 cried while running down the green slope of grass leading into the valley. She held something in her hand.

Zuto still stood there, staring at the point where his father had vanished.

"Zuto . . . the mo-mo-moment has arrived!" Super Media 2.0 said and stood next to him. "It seems as though the end of the world is upon us!"

"What?" Zuto said and raised his eyes towards the sky. A black cloud covered it gradually.

"A mon-monster emerged from the cocoon," said Super Media 2.0, "and the sky is growing da-da-darker. Golden Fortress is collapsing and can't fight it. Silver Shield told us that. Here, he's over t-the-there!" She pointed at the horizon. Silver Shield was there, riding towards them, and Newton sat behind him. "They say if we don't act with determination," she continued, "our world will be de-de-de-" Super Media 2.0 took a deep breath and said slowly, "destroyed."

Zuto didn't know what to say.

"Look what I brought you," she said and gave him the bundle that she held in her hand. It was a black cloak, a bit battered and torn. "I found it in the Recycle Bin. After all, you're like a superhero now; you n-n-need a cloak. That's how it is in the movies."

"But I'm not a superhero," Zuto replied and hung his head. "My father couldn't teach me a thing."

"Where is your father?" she asked.

"All he did was demonstrate how he leaps, and runs, and shoots lightning bolts, just like Silver Shield told us, and then he disappeared." Zuto lifted his head and watched the darkening sky worriedly.

"Try wearing the cloak anyway," requested Super Media 2.0.

Zuto tied the cloak around his neck. In the absence of a mirror, he tried bending down so that he could see it fluttering between his legs; then he straightened up, looking at the cloak over his right shoulder and then over his left.

"You look great," said Super Media 2.0.

The torn fringes of the cloak fluttered in the light breeze. Suddenly, Zuto felt new powers flow through his body.

"What did your father dem-demonstrate to you? Show me," asked Super Media 2.0.

"He started by jumping," said Zuto, "like this." Zuto jumped, almost effortlessly, and disappeared into the sky. After some time, he reappeared and landed with a crash.

"That was a-amazing!" said Super Media 2.0, and helped him to his feet. "Are you okay?"

"Yes," said Zuto wonderingly. "Maybe I did learn something after all." He examined his feet. "I'll try to run too," he added and broke into a run around the valley. He managed to move his feet with tremendous speed, effortlessly, just like his father. He flew, and his black cloak flapped behind him wildly. Finally, he returned to the center of the valley and flung his hands towards the boulders as he ran. A bolt of blue lightning emerged from each hand and smashed the boulders. An awestruck Zuto fell and rolled on the ground, until he found himself lying on his back amidst rock slivers.

"Very nice," said Silver Shield, who had just arrived at the valley together with Newton. "I see you're ready— and just in time. We need your help now."

Zuto rose and stared at his hands.

"The monster wants to destroy Golden Fortress," said Newton, "and then crash the Firewall. That way, the thousands of little worms that hatched from the cocoon will be able to go back to sea and invade other worlds. In the chaos created, we won't be able to stop the worst from happening. The computer will be formatted and our world will meet its end."

"Golden Fortress won't be able to defeat this monster," added Silver Shield. "He didn't prepare for this threat as he should've, and his army will collapse like a house of cards. If we stand aside doing nothing, there's no doubt that Newton's predictions will come true."

The four friends stood staring at each other excitedly. They all realized what a difficult and desperate hour this was, but instead of fear, they were filled with elation, determination, and calm. They stood in a circle and embraced each other.

"The world that threw us to the Recycle Bin n-needs us now," said Super Media 2.0 tremulously. "Let's prove to them who we really are."

"Yes. This is the chance I've been waiting for, like my father before me," said Zuto. "The chance we've all been waiting for."

"I'll take your picture one last time before we leave for battle," Super Media 2.0 said and took several steps backward.

The three friends stood in a row for a group photo.

"It suddenly occurred to me that you never appear with us in the pictures," said Zuto. "That will be the first thing to set right if we win this battle."

"I-I ag-agree," Super Media 2.0 smiled.

"Let's go, friends," said Silver Shield. "The time is short. Follow me."

Chapter 13

While the four friends prepared for a desperate attempt to save the world, the situation deteriorated. A new message appeared now on Tom's computer screen, issued by Golden Fortress, his new anti-virus: "The computer worm cannot be removed. Please disconnect from the Internet to prevent contamination of other computers. Hard drive formatting is advised."

"Dad," Tom yelled to his father, who was in the other room. "I think we have to format the computer." At the same moment, the computer stopped responding altogether.

"Here's the Central Processing Unit," declared Silver Shield (see Zutopedia). "The largest, most crowded city, the center of the world; and things are worse than I thought."

They stopped at a cliff overlooking the enormous metropolis. The city didn't look the same as always. The skies were black, and pillars of fire and smoke could be seen raging on the streets. Instead of the cheerful clatter of machines, factories, and the residents' chatter, all that could be heard were shrieks and explosions.

"Here the fate of our world will be decided," he added. "And upon our shoulders rests the responsibility to try and set things right, if it is not too late."

Sixteen cables passed over their heads, plunged into the abyss beyond the cliff, and twisted over the city streets until they disappeared over the horizon.

"That's the Data Bus," said Newton (see Zutopedia). "It crosses the world, transporting bits from one end to the other. We can use it to quickly arrive at the city center. Jump on one of the zero bits; it's easier to hold on to them."

Only then did Zuto notice Newton was carrying that wooden box from the field in the Recycle Bin.

"Why did you bring the box with you?" wondered Zuto.

"Why not?" answered Newton. "One never knows when one will need a box."

Zuto shrugged.

"It's time to say goodbye to the motorcycle," said Silver Shield. "I can't take it with me any further, and I guess there's no need for it anymore." He rode a short distance from where they stood, and laid the motorcycle on the ground. He gazed upon it sadly and sent a trembling hand to the red button installed on the dashboard. Suddenly, he changed his mind and quickly withdrew his hand. Then he took a deep breath and tried to muster his courage. "No choice . . . no choice . . . ," he muttered to himself, closed his eyes, and once again reached for the red button. He pressed it and a rhythmic beeping started. Silver Shield returned to the group.

"What's the red button for?" asked Zuto.

"Self-destruction," explained Silver Shield, just as the motorcycle exploded into pieces. "Goodbye," the tough anti-virus whispered and wiped a tear.

"Once again, I'm for-for-forced to say: 'I told you so,'" Super Media 2.0 whispered to Zuto. "Eventually, all my fears come true."

"So it seems," Zuto admitted thoughtfully.

"I'll jump first," said Silver Shield, and that's what he did. He hung on a passing zero-bit, just as Newton had told them to, and disappeared beyond the cliff.

Zuto rushed to jump after him.

"Come on, Newton," said Super Media 2.0. "I'll go last."

"Uhhhh," said Newton. Now that it was his turn, fear seized him. Only he and Super Media 2.0 remained there, and she was watching him, so he had no choice. He jumped and disappeared as well.

Super Media 2.0 jumped last and plunged into the abyss while grasping her zero-bit. She closed her eyes in fear during the plunge, which seemed to go on forever. Then she opened them again and found herself hovering above the city houses with her three friends hovering before her. Slightly encouraged, she took another picture.

"Here!" Silver Shield yelled after they'd been floating for a while. "Let's get off here."

They all heard him and landed, one by one, inside a large square.

The skies were gloomy and the city dark. The air was filled with smoke, making it hard to breathe. All around, screaming droves of residents fled, horrified by the monster. No one noticed the four lunatics who chose to hold their ground instead of running away.

"There's Golden Fortress' residence," said Silver Shield.

The fortress towered nearby, its turrets overlooking the square. It seemed defeated now, its flags burnt and its gates broken. Of the vast army of planes that had been buzzing above at Silver Shield's last visit, only a few remained now, hovering aimlessly in the air.

"The situation seems very grave," said Silver Shield. "I think I'll pop inside for a visit and check on my colleague."

"I'll join you," said Newton. "I have a feeling that my skills may be needed there."

The two walked through the broken gate, while Zuto and Super Media 2.0 remained standing on the street by themselves.

"Should we wait for them here?" asked Zuto.

"I don't th-ink there's time," she answered. "We have to search for the mon-mon-monster and try to stop it before it's too late.

"Excuse me," Super Media 2.0 said, approaching one of the residents fleeing past them. "Do you kn-kno- do you kn-"

But he ignored her and continued his hurried escape.

"There's no need to ask them," said Zuto. "All we have to do is go against the flow."

They started walking, glancing around apprehensively.

"I wonder if it is still possible to fix this world," Zuto said as he stared at the chaos surrounding them, "even if we do defeat the monster."

"We can't lose hope now," Super Media 2.0 said, and they kept on walking.

"I hear something," she said suddenly, and they stopped to listen.

The air was rife with shrieks and the pounding of running feet, but among all the commotion, they managed to discern a deep, repeated growl that shook the ground.

"It's coming from over there," Super Media 2.0 called and pointed at a nearby street.

They dashed up the street and in the corner they saw the monster, black and tall, its mouths burning hot and smoking. It marched quickly, trampling and crushing those unlucky enough to cross its path.

Silver Shield and Newton entered the fortress through the broken gate and walked across the white stone hall towards the elevator.

"Just as I expected; the elevator's out of order," said Silver Shield when he saw the elevator's smashed doors. "Another ominous sign."

"Let's try the stairs," Newton said, pointing to a gloomy entrance nearby.

They climbed up many flights until they stopped to sit and rest a bit at the tenth floor. Newton looked up and his heart fell. The staircase seemed to go on forever.

"How many floors does this stupid fortress have?" he complained.

"We don't have to climb all the way up," answered Silver Shield. "We just need to get to the gigantic head's hall."

"And where is that?" asked Newton.

"I can't remember," Silver Shield admitted and peeked through the entrance that led to the tenth floor.

"We're in luck!" he exclaimed. "It's right here!"

Silver Shield and Newton entered Golden Fortress' marble hall. The gigantic head still stood on its wooden podium at the end of the hall, but his eyes were closed.

"The floor is crawling with worms!" stated Newton in disgust. Hundreds of them crept on the marble floor.

"Don't be afraid," said Silver Shield, trampling several of the worms under his feet. "They're still too small to be dangerous. We have to make our way to the head."

"Dangerous or not," answered Newton, "I think it's your job to clear the way. I'll follow your lead."

The two of them continued walking, Silver Shield first, clearing the way with his feet and sword, and Newton close behind him.

Suddenly, the head opened its mouth to speak.

"Is that you, Silver Shield?" he said in a weak, trembling voice, his eyes still closed. "I can no longer see."

"Yes," answered Silver Shield. "What happened here?"

"My army collapsed when faced with the power of that ... creature ... that emerged from the cocoon. It passed by some time ago and destroyed the place. Having no other choice, I issued a message to the user recommending a complete formatting of the computer. This will probably be my last deed."

"Let's not give up hope just yet, Golden Fortress," said Silver Shield. "We brought reinforcements."

"It's too late for me, I'm afraid," the head answered slowly. "I was too proud ... and arrogant...." He choked and coughed. "Now, I must pay the price," he managed to add. A frown wrinkled his forehead as if he was making an enormous effort, and for a moment, his large head seemed to shrink. Then they heard a loud explosion, and the gigantic head disintegrated to pieces and crumbled all over the floor.

Silver Shield shook his head sadly.

"Now, only the four of us remain to stand against the monster," he said morosely, "and the user already got a recommendation to destroy our world completely. Do you think there's any hope left, Newton?"

The monster stood at a crossroads, sniffing the air, trying to decide which way to go. Zuto and Super Media 2.0 looked at it from around a corner. Even though Silver Shield had described the monster to them, they were paralyzed with fear at the sight of its enormous size, black scales, and the smoke that billowed from its four maws.

"It must be searching for the machines that provide power to the Firewall," Super Media 2.0 whispered after she pulled herself together. "We have to st-st-stop it before it has time to find them."

"Should I simply step forward and attack it?" asked Zuto, wondering where he'd draw the courage to do that.

"It's customary to declare something first," replied his friend. "Something such as 'prepare to d-d-die, evil Sea Monster!' That's how it is in the movies."

"Ahm, ahm," Zuto cleared his throat. "Ah . . . ah . . . my voice is too faint," he said finally. "It won't even notice me. Maybe you'll say it?"

"Me?" she asked, surprised. "But I stut-stut-stutter."

Suddenly, one of the monster's heads turned in their direction.

"There's no time for declarations now," said Zuto. He bent his knees slightly and threw his hands forward. Blue lightning shot out of them and hit the monster's head. The blast knocked the head back and sent it hurtling to the ground. A large burn appeared on its neck.

The monster turned its three other heads towards them in a fury. It opened its three fiery maws at them and spat great flames of fire.

"Run!" Zuto shouted and the two jumped, each to a different side of the street. A black hole of soot gaped in the ground where they had been.

The monster leapt on Zuto and tried to trample him. Zuto jumped up high and landed on the roof of an eight-story building nearby. From this vantage point he reassessed the situation and planned another attack. The monster froze, surprised by the agility of the little green creature. The burn seared its body terribly, and it seethed with fury. Zuto flung his hands forward and shot another bolt of lightning at the monster. It leapt aside to avoid it, and started climbing up the wall towards him. Now it was Zuto's turn to be surprised.

The monster shot another barrage of flames at him. He escaped, jumping on the roof of the neighboring building. A new wave of fire almost consumed him, and he ran as fast as he could, jumping from roof to roof. With tremendous leaps that shook the ground, the monster pursued him. If it were not for his new powers, Zuto would have been burned immediately or trampled under the monster's enormous feet.

Completely exhausted, Zuto managed to return to the first building and sneak in through one of the windows.

He hoped to rest there a bit, but the monster didn't give up. It leapt onto the roof of the building with all its weight, and the two upper floors collapsed with an awful crash. Then it jumped back to the street, turned its four heads towards the ruined building, and threw horrifying flames of fire at it again and again. The building went up in flames and collapsed in a heap.

"Oh, no!" Super Media 2.0 mumbled in shock.

The monster shot one last hail of fire, and the blackened pile of metal and stone crumbled to ash.

Silver Shield and Newton still stood in the destroyed hall that had served as Golden Fortress' lavish house and tried to figure out their next move.

"First of all," said Newton, placing the box that he still held in his hand on the floor, "we must send the user a new message, canceling the previous one about formatting the computer. Otherwise, he might begin the process while we're working here."

"For that, we need the Operating System," Silver Shield said and pulled the walkie-talkie from his belt. "Operating System, over! Operating System, over!" he called into the walkie-talkie.

Silence.

"They aren't answering," he said and his face fell. "Maybe the monster already got to them."

"Try again," suggested Newton.

"Operating System, over! Operating System, over!"

Silence.

And suddenly they heard a faint voice that seemed to come from far away: "Umm, yeah . . . who's speaking?"

"We're talking from the Golden Fortress," Silver Shield said loudly. "We have to issue a message to the user. Who's this?"

"This is . . . uh . . . the Operating System. . . ." answered the confused voice from the other side. "But everyone ran away. I'm the only one left. You're speaking with the garbage collector" (see Zutopedia).

"The only one there is some cleaning guy," Silver Shield whispered worriedly to Newton. "I hope he'll be able to do what we ask him to."

"Listen carefully," Silver Shield said, continuing to speak into the walkie-talkie. "This is very important. The fate of the world depends on it. Can you issue a message to the user?"

"Let me check," answered the garbage collector. "There's a manual here explaining how to do it . . . please wait." They waited patiently for a while and then the voice said, "All right. Okay, I can try . . . what's the message you want to pass on to the user?"

Silver Shield dictated the message to the garbage collector, who wrote it down.

"All right," said the garbage collector. "I think I managed to pass on the message. I guess I'll run away now too . . . good luck to you. . . ." And he disconnected.

"I have an idea," said Newton suddenly. "Why don't we hook you up to all these wires." He pointed to the wires that had previously been connected to the gigantic head and now dangled uselessly from the wall. "Maybe you can control Golden Fortress' remaining army?"

"A very interesting idea," answered Silver Shield. "I'd like to try it."

The silver robot stood in the center of the podium, and Newton connected wire after wire to his head.

"Do you feel anything?" asked Newton.

"No," replied Silver Shield.

"Hmmm," said Newton. "I thought you would sense the remaining planes and tanks. This is strange and disappointing."

"Maybe the contacts are loose?" tried Silver Shield.

"No. I connected them properly," Newton answered and glanced around. "A-ha!" he said, "Maybe something broke down in this cabinet!"

He walked towards a cabinet set in the wall, behind the podium, and opened it. Dozens of yellowish worms fell out.

Newton recoiled. "Yuck, disgusting! Silver Shield, come over here and take care of these revolting creatures!"

"But I'm attached to all these wires," replied the anti-virus, who couldn't even turn his head to glance at the cabinet. "Step on them yourself."

"All right," said Newton, grimacing. "I guess that in order to save the world I can trample a few disgusting worms."

He crushed the worms and kicked them away. Then, he turned to see what was going on inside the cabinet. "Yes!" he declared. "Just as I thought! The problem is in here."

Some of the wires in the cabinet had been shredded by the worms' sharp and tiny teeth, while others were simply torn out of place. Disgusting saliva dripped down from the cabinet. Newton wrinkled his nose and muttered incoherent words, but set out to work on the task. He cleaned everything and then connected the wires back in place.

"Hey!" exclaimed Silver Shield suddenly. "I can feel them!"

"What do you feel?" asked Newton, clapping excitedly.

"Seven planes!" declared Silver Shield happily. "And three tanks. I see what they see! And I can move them too!"

"So that's what's left of Golden Fortress' magnificent army," said Newton. "I wonder if that's enough."

"Don't worry," said Silver Shield confidently. "I'll search for Zuto and join forces with him." He closed his eyes and concentrated.

Chapter 14

While Tom wondered what to do next, a new message popped up on his screen:

"Please ignore the previous message. The problem with the worm is still being dealt with. Do not format anything."

"What is going on here?" Tom asked himself in amazement.

Super Media 2.0 stared through her tears at the monster walking away, dragging its feet. She knelt at the street corner and cried next to the pile of ashes, which was, so it seemed, Zuto's grave. Suddenly she heard a strange, metallic rattling noise.

"What was that?" Super Media 2.0 turned her head in alarm.

A roundish metal lid set in the pavement rose slightly, and Zuto's head peeped out.

"Zuto!" Super Media 2.0 cried and burst into a sobbing laughter. "Are you okay?" she asked while helping him out of the narrow hole. "I thought you were dead." She started brushing off the ashes that covered his greenish body with her hands.

"Almost," answered Zuto. "When I heard the roof of the building collapse, I jumped into the garbage chute in the corner of the room. I fell and fell into the darkness. And then, the flames came and engulfed me. I could barely breathe. Suddenly, I hit something hard and cold. I guess I fell into an underground sewer. I heard explosions and the ground trembled, and I knew that the building had collapsed on top of me. I was afraid to move. Later, when it was quiet again, I realized that the monster had gone away, so I started feeling my way through the darkness. It was like a labyrinth, and I almost got lost." He shivered at the thought. "But suddenly I found a tunnel leading upward. I climbed it until I reached this lid."

"Well done!" said Super Media 2.0. "Well done, Zuto!"

"No . . . no . . ." said Zuto in a weak, trembling voice. "It wasn't so well done. The monster is too strong for me. I failed. I guess I wasn't destined for great things after all."

"Forget the mon-monster for now. It's not important. The main thing is that you're a-alive," whispered Super Media 2.0.

Zuto mumbled something and then fainted. Super Media 2.0's heart plummeted, and she remained sitting silently, curled up against the wall.

Suddenly, she opened her green eyes and started playing again that melody that she had played at the lake, long ago. Soft, gentle sounds filled the air and the ruined street. Zuto woke up and blinked. A sunbeam broke forth through the black cloud, illuminating them.

"Here comes the light again," whispered Super Media 2.0. "Whenever things look hopeless, som-something unexpected comes along and brings back hope. That's how it is in the movies."

Just then, they heard a familiar buzz. A golden plane passed above.

"G . . . Golden Fortress' army!" cried Super Media 2.0 joyfully, getting up so she could see better. Another plane flew overhead, and then another, and another, flying towards the monster. "It's still fun-functioning! It's Silver Shield and Ne-Ne-Newton! They did it! You see . . . I told you!"

Encouraged, Zuto got up.

"But that's not enough," he said. "We have to think of some plan."

"The monster thinks you're dead," answered Super Media 2.0 wisely. "We can u-use that to our advantage."

Never before had Zuto felt the horror of death as strongly as he had during his last encounter with the monster. But he was determined to try and finish what he had started.

"What do you suggest?" he asked.

"Go and hi-hide by the fortress. I'll approach the monster and lead it to the fortress, and there, you'll ambush it. Golden Fortress' planes will dis-dis-distract it, and perhaps we'll fi-find more planes near the fortress."

"Do you mean you'll act as bait to catch the monster?" asked Zuto. "Are you crazy?"

"We don't have a choice, Zuto," answered Super Media 2.0 bravely. "I'm the only one left here with you."

Zuto gazed at her quietly. "Turns out you're not a scaredy-cat at all," he said. She smiled at him and disappeared around the corner.

Super Media 2.0 approached the monster. Golden Fortress' seven planes now circled the skies and shot their arrows towards the four writhing heads, but the monster shook them off as if they were pesky flies and continued its march.

Super Media 2.0 took a deep breath and stood in the middle of the street, blocking the monster's way.

"You cannot pass!" she hollered at the top of her voice and waved her hands in the air.

The monster stared in surprise at the little figure.

"I'm Super Media 2.0," the figure continued, "friend of Lightning-Shooting Zuto. The fiery breath will not avail you, Sea Monster!"

The monster remembered the black-haired companion of the green creature who had assaulted it before. The lightning the green creature had shot at it still burned its black flesh.

"Go back to the abyss!" shouted Super Media 2.0.

The monster opened its four maws and released a roar. The earth trembled and the air burned as hot as a furnace.

Super Media 2.0's eyes hurt from the heat and the smoke. She wiped the sweat off her forehead.

"You shall not pass!" she shouted, and her voice echoed down the street.

The monster charged at her furiously, and Super Media 2.0 broke into a sprint and ran towards the fortress.

"Is she crazy?" exclaimed Silver Shield suddenly. He had been observing the monster through the planes he controlled from Golden Fortress` hall. "It's Super Media 2.0! She just came up to the monster and started shouting. What's gotten into her?"

"Perhaps they're planning an ambush," Newton responded and straightened the wires that surrounded the silver anti-virus. "Let the monster follow her, but don't let it get too close."

Silver Shield directed his planes to spin faster around the monster's heads, which slowed it down and allowed Super Media 2.0 to maintain a safe distance. The confused monster's heads breathed fire in every direction, and two of the planes crashed in flames into the street.

Super Media 2.0 ran and ran until she was almost fainting. Suddenly, she saw the fortress turrets rising behind the adjacent buildings, and she raced there with what little strength she had left. She crossed the square, and on the threshold of the ruined fortress gate, she collapsed in exhaustion, her hair ribbons scattering around her. Through the sweat, tears, and hair that covered her eyes, she could see the monster running towards her, opening its four fiery maws.

The monster approached quickly, ready to shoot a hail of fire and eliminate the little pest once and for all. But then a powerful bolt of lightning hit it from the side. It was Zuto, who was hiding behind a nearby building, full of fighting spirit.

The monster was alarmed for a brief moment and then turned its heads towards the old-new threat. But Zuto had already jumped to the other side of the square and mustered his powers again. Calmer and stronger than ever, he shot another bolt of lightning, which penetrated the thick armor on the monster's body, leaving a gaping hole. Now three of Golden Fortress' tanks joined the battle, commanded by Silver Shield. They shot their heavy spears straight towards the yawning hole in the scaly armor, and the monster started to flee.

Zuto ran to the middle of the square, gathering all his powers. He focused on the monster, raised his hands, and sent one last bolt of lightning. A tremendous bang was heard, rumbling to the ends of the world, and the earth trembled. At the sound of the explosion, porters at all the hundreds of ports paused and lifted their heads in wonder. The driver of the Disk Controller was startled and ran to hide behind his tractor. Workers in the Mathematical Processor and the rest of the cities in the world, along with residents of the Recycle Bin, all stood still and wondered what that terrible noise meant. The monster was torn to shreds that flew into the air and spread all over, leaving only two thousand and forty-eight teeth scattered in the square.

"There," said Zuto, exhausted. "Our task is complete."

Chapter 15

Super Media 2.0 got up and ran to Zuto. They hugged each other for a long time. Newton and Silver Shield came through the fortress gate and joined them. The four of them stood there, gazing silently at each other. More and more of the city's residents crept out of their hiding places and approached the big square to see the remains of the defeated monster. Suddenly Zuto burst into an uproarious, uncontrollable, contagious laughter that quickly infected his friends.

The sky began to clear and the smoke dispersed. Growing throngs of residents returned to the city. They all gathered in the square, and soon it was filled with song and dance. Some of the revelers began collecting the monster's teeth and heaping them by the fortress gate until all two thousand forty-eight teeth were accumulated in a pile. The four friends now stood and stared, astonished at the joyous crowd that grew larger and larger as residents kept streaming in from the nearby streets and alleys.

Suddenly a figure left the crowd and approached them.

"Oh, no!" exclaimed Super Media 2.0. "Hide me, Zuto."

The figure resembled her greatly, but was taller and younger. Super Media 2.0 tried to find shelter behind Zuto, but it was too late.

"Super Media 2.0!" cried the figure. "Super Media 2.0!"

"Hello, Super Media 3.0," said Super Media 2.0 dryly.

Super Media 3.0 rushed to her and began talking enthusiastically with a rapid, unstoppable flow of words.

"Oh, Super Media 2.0, we heard what happened," she said. "Is it true that you took part in the war against the monster? Did you really serve as bait and lead it to the death trap you set up? Wow! Are these its teeth? Way to go! Is it true the world was almost destroyed? That's amazing! Are the rumors true?"

"Ye-es," said Super Media 2.0, suddenly filled with pride. "The four of us did it."

"Oh," replied her younger version, hugging her. "That is so amazing! I absolutely worship you. You've brought honor to our entire family. This is just too wonderful and incredible. Someone should write a book about it. Make a movie. Take a picture—"

"Hey," Zuto suddenly exclaimed. "This is our chance to finally get a picture of the four of us. Will you please take our picture, Super Media 3.0?"

"Of course," she answered and took several steps back. "Strike a pose!"

The four friends stood side by side and hugged.

"I can add all sorts of special effects," said Super Media 3.0. "Increase contrast, balance colors, or apply gamma correction. Or maybe you want a picture that looks like an oil painting, or an antique-looking picture, or a picture with—"

"No, that's not necessary," Super Media 2.0 interrupted her. "Just a s-simple picture, please. There's nothing like the s-simple pictures."

"Okay . . . okay . . . give me a big smile," said Super Media 3.0, and *click*, she blinked and took the picture.

"That's odd," said Silver Shield shortly after.

"What's wrong?" asked Super Media 2.0.

"I was walking through the crowd," he replied, "and I heard rumors saying they're going to turn off the computer because of the mess that took place here."

His words struck her out of the blue. "Oh no!" she said, "but everything's okay now. We have to issue a message to the user that everything's back to normal."

"I already issued a similar message," answered Silver Shield. "But perhaps the user is fed up with all the messages we sent him and has made his decision."

"But why now, wh-when we can finally get on with our lives," Super Media 2.0 said in anger and disappointment, "does this user have to barge in and ruin everything! I ho-ho-hope that there's no truth to the-these rumors."

Newton watched the crowd that now filled the square from one end to the other, and his fondness for speeches stirred him into action.

"I'm going up," he declared, and entered the fortress. A short while later, he appeared on a large balcony above the fortress gate, overlooking the square. With nothing better to do, his friends followed him and stood by his side.

Newton put his box at the front of the balcony and stood on it, excited about this opportunity to give a speech of a lifetime to the enormous crowd gathered there: a full, detailed description of his mathematical theory.

But then, watching the celebrating crowd, he was at a loss for words. Newton suddenly realized that no one would understand his theories. He closed his mouth, and a great loneliness fell upon him.

Super Media 2.0 looked at him sympathetically, as if she could read his mind.

"Don't worry, Newton," she said, squeezing his hand, "we love you e-e-even if we can't understand your theories."

While they were talking, a figure appeared at the other side of the square. It was an Operating System agent wearing a yellow coat. He started crossing the square with vigorous, solemn steps. The crowd stepped aside, clearing the way for him.

"He's on his way here," said Newton. "He probably has a message to deliver."

The agent entered the fortress gate.

"Good," said Super Media 2.0. "We can ask him about the rumors of turning off the computer."

Shortly after, the agent appeared on the balcony, carrying a stack of papers.

"Tell me, please," asked Super Media 2.0 impatiently, "we he-heard rumors that the user is going to tu-tu-turn off the computer. Is there any tru-truth to those rumors?"

"As a matter of fact, it has already happened," replied the agent.

"What?!" said Super Media 2.0. "But how can that be? We're all s-still here, aren't we?"

"Listen to my message and it will all become clear," replied the agent.

He walked to the front of the balcony and tried to silence the bustling crowd.

"The com-com-computer can't be turned off," Super Media 2.0 said to Zuto, who stood beside her. "Surely he must be mis-mis-mistaken."

Chapter 16

"What's up with your computer?" asked Tom's dad as he entered the room. "Is everything okay?"

"I don't know," answered Tom. "I started getting all kinds of weird messages. 'Format the computer; don't format the computer; there's a worm; there isn't a worm.' I couldn't understand what was going on. Suddenly, the computer got stuck and stopped responding. The last message was: 'Your computer was rescued! Forget everything that has happened!' And then it started working again."

"Weird," said Tom's dad.

"I think the computer was on for too long and it went a little crazy. I turned it off," said Tom and left his room.

"May I stand on the box?" asked the agent, preparing to read his announcement.

"No," replied Newton, who still stood on it himself. He turned to the crowd and called, "Hear ye, hear ye! An announcement from the Operating System."

The agent began his announcement: "I am carrying a missive from the Operating System. Let me assure you that it's coming from the highest source. I will now read it to you." He leafed through the pages he held in his hand and then started reading out loud.

"As you most certainly know, our world has just faced the danger of annihilation and our fate hung by a thread. This is not a myth or an exaggeration. A horrific monster rampaged amongst us, sowing chaos and ruin all around. It destroyed the anti-virus and threatened to crash the Firewall and spread an epidemic in other worlds beyond the sea. For a moment, it seemed as though all of our defenses had failed and that we wouldn't be able to resist it. A message was issued to the user, advising him to format the computer. Total destruction of our world seemed inevitable." The agent paused briefly and a tense silence fell on the square.

"But then, out of nowhere, four heroes arrived," he continued loudly, "and here they are now, standing beside me. While we all wallowed in fear and despair, these four heroes stood alone against the monster, and prevailed!"

Cheers rose from the crowd.

"Therefore, it has been decided to bestow upon each and every one of them a medal from the Operating System," said the agent to the sound of the crowd's wild hoorays and applause. He pulled four golden medals on ribbons from his satchel, and to the crowd's cheers he hung them around the necks of Zuto, Super Media 2.0, Newton, and Silver Shield, who beamed with pride and joy. Then the agent returned to the front of the balcony and continued reading out loud.

"Furthermore, in light of Silver Shield's success in operating Golden Fortress' army, we have decided to keep him in this role until further notice. From now on, he will be called: Golden Shield."

Once again the crowd burst in cheers. Silver Shield . . . that is, Golden Shield blushed and took a bow.

"After many discussions and careful thought," the agent continued, still reading his announcement, "it has been decided not to issue any message to the user regarding this matter, for fear it would only get us into more trouble."

Giggles rose from the gathered crowd.

"And finally, a painful announcement," the agent continued.

"Here it comes," said Super Media 2.0.

"Some time ago, we received an order to turn off the computer. The shut-down process has already begun."

Cries of despair rose from the square.

"So it's true," said Super Media 2.0 sadly.

The agent continued reading the announcement in a quiet voice that shook slightly, but he could be heard clearly in the silence that now ensued.

"Soon darkness will fall on the world, life in it will cease, and time will stand still. Let me remind you that this is a natural occurrence, and a reversible one. In light of the great danger we have just escaped, let us take consolation in the hope that a time will come when our world will be revived. A cleaner world it will be, fresh and renewed, and we will return to live in it, peacefully and joyfully, as we did in the past.

"Our world has existed for more than 500 billion clock cycles. During this time, over two million ships were served at the ports, carrying 16 megabytes" (see Zutopedia) "of information into and out of our world. Over 300 gigabytes were written and read from the Hard

Drive, and about 83 terabytes of information passed through the data bus."

The agent finished reading one page and, with trembling hands, went on to the second.

"I want to thank all of you gathered here in the square, workers and porters, drivers, agents, applications and services, web services, widgets and gadgets, and all the others I may have forgotten. Thank you all for taking part in this tremendous undertaking, the fruit of the efforts of so many working hands.

"Now, we have one final task to complete," the agent added, his voice filled with pride. "We must prepare for the imminent end: clean and tidy up, each of us according to his or her ability and responsibility, and prepare the world for the deep slumber that is about to fall on it. Let us complete this last task too, as best we can, so that we can look back at this age of the world and proudly say: our part is wholly done."

A long and profound silence prevailed. The only sound was the rustle of the agent's papers as he folded them with shaking hands.

"Wonderful speech, sir," Newton said, and started applauding. The crowd joined him and soon everyone was clapping their hands. They applauded the Operating System agent, the four heroes on the balcony, and each other. After the applause died down and was replaced with farewells, the crowd dispersed, going to perform the last task that had been assigned to them.

"Now what?" asked Zuto.

"If you want to save your memory," said Newton, "you have to go to the Disk Controller and store yourselves. If you don't, then you won't remember anything of what happened in this age of our world."

"Oh, no!" said Super Media 2.0. "Let's all hu-hurry up and do that. After all, we can't give up such memories. And the pic-pic-pictures! All the pictures I took! We have to save them all."

"Wait," said Zuto. "What about me? Will I be allowed to store myself?"

"I'm afraid not," said Newton. "You're a virus. You won't be allowed to do that."

"But he's a hero!" protested Super Media 2.0. "He has a me-medal. They'll probably make an ex-exception for him."

The Operating System agent, who was still standing there on the balcony, listened to their conversation.

"The Operating System administration won't even think of it," he said. "As a result of the recent events, whenever they hear the word 'virus,' they immediately run and hide under the table. They'll refuse any request to save any kind of virus."

"Well, then I'll ask to save him for research purposes," said Golden Shield. "I've done that before."

"In calmer times they would've approved such a request easily," answered the agent. "But now, as I've already mentioned, there's an atmosphere of panic. I wouldn't waste time on that kind of request."

Saying that, the agent collected his belongings and left.

"So, is Zuto doomed to lose his memory?" asked Super Media 2.0 sadly.

"Much worse," said Golden Shield. "Zuto is a mutation, and there's no saved copy of him in the Hard Drive. There's no longer any copy of any viruses from Zuto's family. I cleaned them all. I'm afraid that when darkness falls on our world, Zuto will just . . . disappear forever."

"No!" cried Super Media 2.0 and went to hug the green creature, "Zuto!"

"Don't be afraid, Super Media," said Zuto. His gaze was sharp and determined. "Now I know what I have to do."

"What?" she asked.

"I have to run away to sea."

Chapter 17

Strong winds blew at Port 80. One lone ship, the last one to leave the world, moored at the port, and the porters had almost finished loading it. Zuto stood at the bottom of the grassy hill with his friends, who had come to bid him farewell.

"When you return," Golden Shield said to Zuto, "tell me about the journey and the worlds you'll have visited. You'll probably meet strange monsters. I must be aware of what lies overseas."

"I will," promised Zuto, and the two shook hands.

The ship sounded its horn now, a long mournful sound, and started gliding on the water.

"I'll tell them about you over there, Newton," said Zuto. "I'll say that I have a friend who knows the deepest secrets of the world."

"Hmmm," answered Newton. "I haven't told you yet, but I have no intention of saving myself in the Hard Drive. When the user turns off the computer, all my knowledge will be lost."

His friends looked at him with astonishment.

"But why?" asked Super Media 2.0.

"I . . . I . . ." Newton tried to explain, "I . . . have nothing left to aspire to. I have no one to share my theories with. If I lose my memory, at least I'll be able to start anew."

The ship now stopped in front of the Firewall, rocking gently with the waves. It sounded its horn again and waited for the gate to open.

Super Media 2.0 sighed. There was no time left to argue. "Here at last," she said, "on the shores of Port 80, comes the end of our fe-fellowship."

"You must hurry and say your goodbyes," Newton said to Zuto.

Zuto went over to Super Media 2.0 to say goodbye.

"You made your wish come true," she said to him. "You did something worthy. What is more worthy than sav-sav-saving the world?"

"Yes," he answered. "But now I have a new wish."

"What is that?" she asked.

"To return safely . . . ," he replied, "to all the places and friends I love. To you . . ."

"I'll wait for you," promised Super Media 2.0, and the two held each other for a long time.

A gate appeared in the Firewall and began to open.

"Zuto!" Newton called urgently, "there's no time left for emotional farewells. Now, let me give you some final advice."

Zuto took a deep breath.

"Do you see the numbers on the lighthouse?" asked Newton. "132.117.124.117?"

"Yes," answered Zuto.

"That's the IP address" (see Zutopedia) "of our world. You must memorize these numbers. Never forget them, no matter what."

"132.117.124.117 ... 132.117.124.117 ... ," Zuto muttered to himself.

"They're also written on the sides of the ships," continued Newton, pointing at the ship gliding out of the gate. "The ship will take you to another world. Stay there, in the vicinity of the port. After some time, and it might be a very long time, you will see a ship with the writing 'From 132.117.124.117.' That will be a sign that our world has returned to life, and our ports are working again. Only then will you be able to return. Search for a ship with the writing 'To 132.117.124.117,' and sneak onto it. It will bring you here."

"That's what I'll do," said Zuto. "132.117.124.117 ... I'll remember that ... "

The gate of the Firewall had already closed behind the last ship, and it started sailing towards open seas, sounding its horn in farewell.

"Thank you, Newton," said Zuto. "Thank you all . . . for everything . . ."

"You must be on your way, Zuto," said Newton, placing his speech box on the grass. "Use the box as a springboard. Quickly."

Zuto burst into a sprint up the hill. He wasn't the same virus who had performed the stunt with the motorcycle so long ago (a little less than a minute). With the help of his new powers, he now dashed up the hill with tremendous speed, his black cloak fluttering behind him. Then, he leapt on the box and jumped with all his might, flying in the air over the Firewall and landing on the lighthouse. He just had time to wave to his friends, and they waved back. He looked at the departing ship and jumped again.

The friends he left behind, standing on the green hill, managed through the flames of the Firewall to see him land on the ship and disappear into its belly.

Super Media 2.0 and Golden Shield said their farewells to Newton and hurried together to the Disk Controller. The red courtyard buzzed with various creatures who had come to save themselves in the Hard

Drive. One after another, they entered the gate, and a cloud of smoke and sparks turned them into a series of bits that poured into the wagon of one of the tractors. All sixteen tractors were working full throttle now, driven by their blue-overalled drivers, who were rushing back and forth in order to serve all the clients as fast as possible.

"A sad ending," Super Media 2.0 said and wiped away a tear.

"I think," said Golden Shield, "that this is neither a sad nor a happy ending, because this isn't an ending at all. I feel that this is only a beginning. Soon, the user will turn on the computer, and we'll wake up to a more beautiful world."

"Do you think Zuto will ever come back?" she asked. "The sea is dangerous and who knows what kind of pe-pe-perils lie in wait in other worlds. And what if, should he withstand all that, he forgets the address to our world and he can never return? What if he won't want to re-re-return? What if the user doesn't even re-restart the computer? Maybe the user will th-throw the entire com-computer into some huge Recycle Bin?"

"As usual, my dearest Super Media," replied the anti-virus, "you think of the worst."

"Until now, all my fears have c-c-come true," she said.

"Yes. We have been forced to cope with our worst nightmares," admitted Golden Shield, "but we have faced them bravely and prevailed. And that's how it will be in the future as well."

The line gradually grew shorter, until only the two of them were left standing in the now-desolate courtyard. One of the tractors appeared over the hill, and its driver motioned Golden Shield to approach him. The silver robot walked heavily to the gate. The machine was activated and Golden Shield vanished in a cloud of smoke. Then, several thousand bits poured straight into the tractor wagon and it left.

"Goodbye," mumbled Super Media 2.0. She was left there waiting, all alone.

A short while later, another tractor emerged from the green hills. Its driver was the same one who had served them when they restored Zuto's father.

"Hey!" he exclaimed happily, "what an honor it is for you to be the very last one saved on the disk!"

"Yes," she said and smiled.

"And what an honor it is for me to serve you again. Come on, there isn't much time left. Come to the gate."

Super Media 2.0 walked to the gate, and the driver turned on the machine.

Newton climbed up the roof of a high, rusty container near the lake, where he sat, waiting for the end of the world. From a distance, he could hear the Operating System's yellow squad cars patrolling among the cities: "Prepare for the darkening of the world! Prepare for the darkening of the world!"

The skies, which were usually blue, changed their color now to a deep, dark shade of purple.

What a wonderful vantage point from which to watch the end of everything, thought Newton to himself. It's a shame I won't remember this experience.

In the horizon he could see the sea and hundreds of ports, as well as the Firewall guarding them. Just then, while enjoying the picturesque view, Newton saw the Firewall fade and disappear. A profound silence now prevailed. The stir of the Operating System's squad cars came to a stop. The world was almost completely empty of its inhabitants. A pink stripe appeared on the horizon above the sea, and then green and yellow stripes. Soon the entire sky became a spectacular myriad of colors.

Super Media 2.0 should have taken a picture of this, Newton thought.

So deep and absolute was the silence that Newton thought he had lost his hearing completely. Suddenly, the sky became bright, burning red, and Newton noticed the bits stop at the data bus that crossed the horizon behind him. The bits stopped gradually in other cables of the world as well, and one after another they all stood still. Finally, the color of the sky changed to a soft, tranquil gold, and Newton felt as if he was floating on the softest and fluffiest of clouds.

He fell off the container and shattered on the ground.

Then the lights went off and a great darkness descended on the world.

The End

Epilogue

Tom went out to play with his friends and forgot all about what happened between five minutes and twenty-seven seconds past three, and six minutes and twenty-seven seconds past three: the worm, the strange messages, and the computer that got stuck and then started working again. In the evening he watched television with his family, and the next day he went to school as usual. When he returned, he ate a snack and did his homework, went to his judo lesson, and afterwards tried to decide if he wanted to watch television or play on the computer.

Eventually he decided to watch television. He sat in front of it and started changing channels. After several minutes, when he couldn't find anything interesting, he turned it off and sighed. Maybe I'll play on my computer after all, he thought and went to his room.

A great darkness prevailed in the world. Everything was still and frozen.

Suddenly, the lights went on. The blue sky reappeared above, bright and clear, yet beneath it the world was cold and quiet. Signs of life could be seen in only one corner of the Central Processing Unit: several cables were already transporting their first bits.

Three creatures stood in a circle nearby. They looked like the Operating System agents, but they wore red coats.

"What is this cold country?" asked one of them. "And what is our role in it?"

"I think it's a gigantic amusement park," answered another, "designed for our entertainment and pleasure."

"And I think," said the third, "that the world is a riddle, and our task is to study and solve it."

They continued their philosophical discussion of the essence of the world and their role in it for a long time, until suddenly, a fourth agent approached them. He too was wearing a red coat, as well as a large boot on his foot.

"You're supposed to start the computer, you laggards!" he yelled. "Get to work!" He accompanied his words with a kick that launched them far away.

The three agents landed in the Disk Controller's red courtyard. At the sight of the gate, the fence, and the fleet of tractors, they remembered who they were and what they had to do. Hastily, they climbed into the tractors and started harvesting the hill near the fence, bringing the crop to the machine by the gate.

The Disk Controller gate was reactivated, and creatures started emerging from it. First came the Operating System's agents, wearing their yellow coats bearing the words "Operating System" on the back. They started scattering around the world, preparing it for new life: cleaning the dust, activating the machines, and resuming work at the ports.

The data bus resumed its flow, and so did all the other cables in the world, which started warming up again. Now the Disk Controller's regular drivers emerged from the gate in their blue overalls.

The most senior driver, our old acquaintance, got up and approached the red agents driving his tractors.

"Buddies!" he called, "that's it. Your work is done. We'll take over from here."

"Gladly," said the three of them, and they retired to a quiet corner where they calmly continued their philosophical discussion.

Now the fleet of tractors was once again in the hands of the Disk Controller drivers, who were busy restoring all the inhabitants of the world.

Suddenly Super Media 2.0 emerged from the gate. Confused and bewildered, she stood by the Disk Controller's shack and waited.

And then Golden Shield appeared.

"Golden Shield," she exclaimed happily. The two friends ran towards each other and spun together in a circle.

"You see, a new world has been created, just like I said it would," said Golden Shield and took a deep breath. "The air is so clean!"

"Yes," she said and smiled.

"I will now leave for my new position," he said, polishing his gold medal proudly. "You're welcome to visit anytime."

He went on his way, and Super Media 2.0 stayed to wait for Newton. After a while, he came out of the gate too. He looked younger and wasn't wearing the gold medal they had received.

"Hello, Newton," said Super Media 2.0.

"Hello there," he answered, discomfited. "Do we know each other?"

"Not exactly, but we're ne-neighbors. Both of us live in the Recycle Bin. Come, I'll show you," she said, and the two of them went on their way.

Newton and Super Media 2.0 became friends again and spent much time together in the Recycle Bin and the nearby lake. And yet, Super Media 2.0 avoided telling him about the events that had taken place in the world's previous age.

After all, if he wished to lose his memory, she thought, his wishes should be respected.

Most of her time, though, Super Media 2.0 spent waiting at Port 80. She spent so much time there that once, a porter came up to her and asked her what she was doing there.

"I have a be-be-beloved overseas," she said, showing him the only picture of the two of them together. "I'm wai-waiting for him to return."

The porter laughed and went back to work.

Once, she came to the port with Newton. Unusually strong winds were blowing, and many ships arrived at the port and left it. The porters, who by now knew her well, waved hello to her and she waved back. When they passed by the large warehouse, one bit fell off the cable above them straight onto Newton's head and knocked him to the ground. Super Media 2.0 helped him to his feet, and they went to sit and recuperate on the grassy hill overlooking the port.

Newton looked thoughtfully at the cables.

"You know," he said suddenly, "I have an idea."

"What idea?" asked Super Media 2.0.

"All these bits, running there," he said, "there must be some kind of formula that operates them."

"Do you think so?" asked Super Media 2.0.

"Yes," he mumbled, while his thoughts already wandered far away. He got up to leave and suddenly noticed something on the ground.

"Hey!" he exclaimed and went to pick up the object. "A box! This can come in handy."

Super Media 2.0 looked at him and smiled. He mumbled a faint "goodbye" and wandered off, carrying his box. She remained on the hill by herself.

She sat there lonely for a long time. The movement of ships had already stopped, and the port stood empty. Disappointed, she got up to leave.

"Miss!" the porters called to her, and pointed at the horizon. "Miss, another ship is arriving!"

For some reason, Super Media 2.0 was seized with tremendous excitement.

The ship sailed closer, paused at the entrance to the port, and sounded its horn. The gate of the Firewall opened slowly. Super Media 2.0 searched for signs of Zuto on deck, but didn't see a thing except many bits lined up in rows. She sighed and turned to go.

Suddenly she heard someone call her name. She looked at the porters, who had already started unloading the ship, and one of them pointed towards the lighthouse. She turned her head.

Zuto stood there, waving at her, his black cloak flapping in the wind and a gold medal sparkling on his chest.

Laughing and crying, she ran towards him, and he jumped from the lighthouse over the Firewall, landing by her side.

"Well, I'm back," said Zuto, and they fell into each other's arms.

Zutopedia

The truth behind *Zuto: The Adventures of a Computer Virus*.

Visit our homepage: www.zutopedia.com.

Comments are welcome.

Anti-Virus and Firewall

Just as every country needs a police force, border checkpoints, and other means of security, the computer needs these things as well.

The anti-virus is similar to the police. It follows the programs installed on the computer and searches for malicious software, also called *malware* (see entry). The term anti-virus is misleading, because viruses are just one type of malware. There are also other kinds of malware, such as computer worms, and anti-viruses are supposed to fight all of them. They recognize malware according to a list of all the known malware programs, just like identikits of criminals used by the police. New malware programs are being discovered all the time, so this list must be updated every once in a while.

An anti-virus may sometimes suspect a program even if that program doesn't appear on the malware list. For example, if a program tries to attach something to another program, it will raise the anti-virus' suspicion, because this is the way computer viruses usually behave.

The computer also has something similar to a border checkpoint: The Firewall. The Firewall inspects all messages going in and out of the computer through the Internet (see entry), and is allowed to delete messages suspected as dangerous. The Firewall helps defend the computer against the threats posed by the Internet: an attempt to infiltrate malware, an attempt to steal confidential information, an attempt to bomb the computer with dummy messages in order to crash it, and many more.

Bit

Bit means the numeral 0 or 1. At any given moment, billions of bits flow inside the computer through tiny wires. You couldn't see them, though, even if you looked inside the computer with a microscope. This is because they are not drawn the way you draw zeros and ones on a page. Instead, the computer represents bits using electric currents. Whenever an electric current flows through a wire, it means that the bit 1 is flowing through it. And when no current flows through a wire, the bit 0 is flowing through it.

Indeed, all the computer does is process bits (0 or 1): it stores them, moves them from one place to another, and performs various operations on them. With bits you can represent numbers (*see* Decimal and Binary Numeral System), which allows the computer to perform mathematical calculations. Bits can also represent pictures, music, movies, software, and more. The wide variety of things that one can do with a simple "creature" such as a bit is what makes the computer such a powerful tool.

Central Processing Unit

See Chip

Chip

A chip is an electronic circuit in which millions of tiny components are tightly packed in a box only several millimeters in size. Chips are sometimes also called integrated circuits or microchips.

In a typical personal computer there's one big chip called the central processing unit (CPU). This is usually the largest, most expensive, and most sophisticated chip in the computer. It is responsible for most of the computer's work.

The computer also needs additional chips in order to fill all sorts of supporting roles. These chips are called *co-processors*. For example, the mathematical co-processor is responsible for carrying out calculations involving fractional numbers (actually, in modern computers there is no longer a mathematical co-processor. The CPU has taken over this task as well). A *disk controller* is another chip, responsible for the communication with the hard drive (see entry).

The CPU and the other chips in your computer are all installed on a single board called the *motherboard*. Since the chips on the motherboard need to communicate with each other, the motherboard contains an additional component known as the *data bus*. The simplest data bus is actually a collection of 16 or 32 electric wires that cross the motherboard. The chips use the wires to "talk" to each other (actually, they are transmitting bits on the wires. *See* bit).

Clock Cycle

Imagine an orchestra with 100 musicians playing a musical piece. Now imagine that each of them is playing to his or her own rhythm, disregarding the other players. Obviously, it would sound terrible. Therefore, in real life, every orchestra has a conductor, who sets one tempo for all the musicians. This guarantees that the bass player on the far right will play in unison with the violin player on the far left, and so will all the others.

Now imagine a computer with millions of components, each one of them responsible for performing a certain task. Each component receives bits (see entry), performs certain operations on them, passes the result to other components, and then receives more input bits, performs operations on them, passes on the result, and so on. What would happen if each component worked at its own rate? Utter chaos!

For this reason, the computer has a clock that is like the conductor of an orchestra. This clock periodically sends signals to all the millions of components. When a component receives a signal it means it must finish its current operation, pass on the result, and prepare for new input bits to arrive. A modern computer should work at a rate of billions of signals per second. The time period passing between two of these signals is called a clock cycle.

So what is the best length for a clock cycle? Let's assume that the clock cycle is set to one-tenth of a second, meaning that a signal is sent to the components ten times a second. This is a very slow tempo for the computer components, and they'll simply work slowly. If we gradually reduce the clock cycle, the rate of the signals will increase and the computer will accelerate its operations. And what happens if the clock cycle is too short? The rate of the signals will be too fast, which may raise two problems. First, some of the components will not have time to complete their tasks during the short period of time given to them, which will result in an accumulation of calculation errors. Second, the increased speed will overheat the components and they will burn (this isn't a metaphor. The computer will go up in flames and might burn the house down).

The clock rate is measured in units called *hertz*, named after the German physician Heinrich Hertz. If the clock works at a rate of one hertz, it means one signal per second. A typical personal computer works at a rate of three gigahertz (*see* Large Numbers), which means three billion signals per second.

Data Bus

See Chip

Decimal and Binary Numeral System

Let's imagine that you owe your friend twelve dollars, and you want to write it down in your diary so that you won't forget. There are many ways to write the number of dollars you owe. One way is to simply write it by using the English word *twelve*, meaning you'll write "I owe my friend *twelve* dollars."

Another, completely different way is to use special markings. For example, you can write "I owe my friend IIIIIIIIIIII dollars." Each *I* represents the number one. To figure out how many dollars you owe, you simply need to count the *I*'s. This method is called the *unary numeral system*. Even though it is an ancient system, it's still used today, especially by people who need to quickly count something on a blackboard. Of course, this system becomes tiring if you need to write large numbers.

A more sophisticated system is the *Roman numeral system*. In addition to the *I* symbol that represents one, this system has other symbols; for example, *V* represents five and *X* represents ten. If you choose to use this system, you will write "I owe my friend XII dollars."

An even more sophisticated system is the *decimal numeral* system. This is the familiar way of writing numbers using the digits 0, 1, 2, 3, 4, 5, 6, 7, 8, 9. Using this system, you will write in your diary "I owe my friend 12 dollars." In this system, the position of the digits is very important. If you accidentally write "I owe my friend 21 dollars," you may have used the same digits, yet you wrote a larger number. Another thing that makes this system so sophisticated is the clever use of the digit 0. Even though by itself 0 means nothing, if you write "I owe my friend 120 dollars," then the debt becomes ten times higher.

One might wonder why there are exactly ten digits: 0, 1, 2, 3, 4, 5, 6, 7, 8, 9. Why not nine digits, or eleven? The number of digits was chosen because humans have ten fingers on their hands. Actually, the word *digit* also means *finger,* a reminder of how this system evolved. Therefore, using ten digits is just an historical human preference. You can create a similar numeral system with any number of digits you want.

Computers use the *binary numeral system*, a numeral system very similar to the decimal numeral system, even though it has only two digits: 0 and 1 (sometimes called bits, see entry). The two digits have their usual meaning: 0 means nothing and 1 means one, but similar to the decimal system, the position of the digits can change the number dramatically. Every time you add an additional 0 to a number, the number is doubled. For example, in the binary numeral system, the number 10 means two, 100 means four, 1000 means eight, and so on. Twelve in binary is written like this: 1100, which is eight (1000) and four (100) added together.

Therefore, if you choose to use the binary numeral system, you would write in your diary "I owe my friend 1100 dollars." Actually, you'd better make a note that this number is written in binary: "I owe my friend 1100 (binary number) dollars." Otherwise you might accidentally think 1100 was written in the decimal numeral system, in which it means *one thousand and one hundred* instead of *twelve*. Knowing what system a number was written in is very important in order to read it correctly.

To understand more about how the binary and decimal numeral systems work, see http://www.zutopedia.com.

Easter Eggs

During the Christian holiday of Easter, it's customary to color eggs, hide them in various places, and send the children searching for them.

In software the term *Easter eggs* means hidden features, usually ones that programmers added as a joke.

Easter eggs are hidden in many famous software applications. For example, in Microsoft Word 97, a word processing software, the programmers hid a complete pinball game. The game is well hidden: to activate it you must follow a long list of secret instructions.

Firewall

See Anti-Virus and Firewall

Garbage Collector

Imagine two kids, Alice and Bob, playing with their toys, each in his own room. Alice is tidy. She picks one toy from her drawer and plays with it on the carpet. When she is done, she carefully puts the toy back in the drawer. Her room remains neat at all times.

Bob, on the other hand, is not that tidy. Whenever he finishes playing with a toy, he simply leaves it lying on the floor. After a few hours of play the entire carpet becomes cluttered with toys, and there is no more room to play at all. Every time this happens, his father steps in and puts all the toys back in the drawers and cabinets. Bob can then continue playing on the now clear carpet, and he starts cluttering it with toys all over again.

Surprisingly, both types of behavior can be found among computer programs. All programs need memory space in order to store stuff when they are running, much like kids put toys on the carpet in their room when they are playing. Tidy programs keep their memory space neat: whenever they are done with something they erase it. Sloppy programs, just like Bob, don't erase anything by themselves, and soon enough they run out of memory.

This is when the Garbage Collector steps in. The Garbage Collector cleans all the unused stuff and frees up memory so that the sloppy program may continue running.

You might now think that sloppy programs are bad, and that the programmers who wrote them should be fired. This is not the case at all. In fact, some computer languages, like a famous one named Java, were especially designed to work with a garbage collector. This makes life easier for the programmers, who don't need to worry about cleaning up the resources their programs use. Such languages are not called sloppy; they are simply called *garbage-collected languages.*

Hard Disk Drive (or Hard Drive)

Everybody knows computers are electronic machines. They need electricity. If you disconnect a computer from a power supply, it will shut down immediately. Not only that, but the computer will also "forget" everything: all the photos, games, movies, and songs stored in its memory will be lost. The computer memory, you see, also needs electricity, so when you cut off the power, everything is erased.

Well, not exactly everything. The computer has one component especially designed *not* to require electricity: the hard drive. This special property of hard drives makes them useful for storing stuff for long periods of time, years even. The files you have on your personal computer at home, all the photos, games, movies, and songs, are all stored in your computer's hard drive. Just like in any other part of the computer, information is saved as a series of bits (see entry).

Here is a game that will help explain how hard drives work, and why they don't need electricity. Imagine eight coins lined up in a row on the table. Each coin showing heads will represent 0, and each coin showing tails will represent 1. These coins are like a simple hard drive, and they can store numbers! For example, let's say we want to store the number 12 (perhaps as a reminder we owe someone twelve dollars). First we need to convert the number to binary representation (see Decimal and Binary Numeral System), which turns out to be 00001100. Therefore, we will arrange the coins this way: heads, heads, heads, heads, tails, tails, heads, heads. That's it! Our coin-hard-drive now stores the number twelve, and it will continue to do so until we will choose to store a different number. Storing a new number is easy: we simply flip the coins again to match the binary representation of the new number. If you write and erase numbers with pencil and eraser over and over again, sooner or later the paper will become dirty and worn out. Not so with our coin-hard-drive: we can flip the coins over and over again, to store whatever number we choose!

In real life, hard drives don't contain coins, but billions of tiny magnetic particles. The drive has a sensor that can detect the direction of their magnetic fields, and flip them over, just like the coins on the table.

The magnetic particles are usually divided into sectors; each sector can store 4,096 bits. The number of sectors can reach hundreds of millions. Therefore, the hard drive can store billions and even trillions of bits (usually referred to as Gigas and Teras. *See* Large Numbers).

Hexadecimal Numbers

We can write the same number in many different ways (see Decimal and Binary Numeral System). When programming a computer, one often bumps into a strange numeral system known as hexadecimal (or base 16). This system uses the usual ten digits 0, 1, 2, 3, 4, 5, 6, 7, 8, 9 but also uses the letters A, B, C, D, E, F as additional digits, resulting in a total of sixteen digits. Numbers written in hexadecimal may be any combination of those digits, for example: 12A3, BC10, ABCD, 450, 15FFF30.

The hexadecimal system is used because it is easier to translate it to the binary system used by the computer. To understand more about how it works, see http://www.zutopedia.com.

Internet

Before the Internet was invented, there were smaller networks known as *local area networks*, or LANs. For example, if some company wanted all the computers in its office building to be able to communicate with each other, it installed a LAN in the building. This allowed an employee in one office to chat with an employee in another office in the same building. However, there was no communication possible with computers outside the building, and definitely not in other cities or other countries.

The idea behind the Internet was simple: to connect all the existing small networks to each other in order to create one large network. This explains why the Internet is called *Internet:* when we want to say that something is related to many nations, we say that it's international. When we want to say that something's composed of many networks, we say: Inter-net.

Let's say a kid in the USA wants to send an email to a friend in China. Of course those two kids` computers are not connected directly, but they are both connected to the Internet! Therefore this email will be able to travel from one computer to the other, though it will have a long, fantastic journey, crossing many different kinds of networks. It may travel through optical fibers and copper wires, and even be shot to a satellite in space and back again to earth. All of this of course may take less than a second.

Through these multitudes of networks, your computer at home is connected to approximately one half-billion (*see* Large Numbers) computers that make up the Internet.

IP Address

The Internet (see entry) is composed of thousands of networks and millions of computers. Since it has such a complicated structure, a clever set of rules was invented in order to define how the computers would communicate with each other. This set of rules is called Internet Protocol, or IP for short.

According to the Internet Protocol, each computer receives an address called an IP address, consisting of four numbers. An IP address might look like this, for example: 132.117.214.117. An IP address is similar to a phone number. You must know your friend's phone number if you want to give him a call, right? Similarly, if a computer needs to send a message to a distant computer, it needs the distant computer's IP address.

There is another striking similarity between IP addresses and phone numbers. If you want to call some guy, say, Robinson Crusoe, but you don't know his phone number, can you obtain his number somehow? Yes, of course. You can look up his name in a phone directory! A phone directory has an alphabetical list of many people's names, together with their phone numbers. Similarly, some (but not all) computers have a name, in addition to an IP address. These names usually look something like: www.somecomputer.foo.

There are also special directories for looking up the IP address of a computer by its name. Such a directory is called a DNS (domain name server). Every time you surf the Internet and go to a site, for example www.wikipedia.org, the first thing that happens is that your computer looks up www.wikipedia.org's IP address in a DNS. Using the IP address, it can then communicate with this computer and retrieve the content of the site.

Large Numbers

You are no doubt familiar with the numbers one thousand (1,000) and one million (1,000,000). You probably also know large numbers such as one billion (1,000,000,000) and one trillion (1,000,000,000,000).

Surely you've also heard words such as *kilo*, *mega*, and *giga*. People use them all the time. For example, someone might say, "My new computer has two gigabytes of memory," without even knowing what *gigabyte* means. It is enough for most people that *giga* sounds impressive.

Actually *kilo*, *mega*, and *giga* are very simple to explain. *Kilo* means *one thousand*, *mega* means *one million*, and *giga* means *one billion*. What's special about them is that you can combine them with another word and create a new word. For example, *kilometer* means *one thousand meters*, *megagram* means *one million grams*, and *gigasecond* means *one billion seconds*.

Kilo, *mega*, and *giga* are prefixes. They come to us from Greek. Here's a table with the four smallest prefixes:

Prefix	Meaning of the word in Greek	Number
Kilo	One thousand	1,000
Mega	Big	1,000,000
Giga	Huge	1,000,000,000
Tera	Monstrous	1,000,000,000,000

Computer engineers adopted these prefixes to describe various properties of the computer, but here comes a twist. A number like 1,000 might seem like a nice, round number to you, but not to a computer engineer. A computer engineer would much prefer the number 1,024 over 1,000. This is because 1,024 is a power of 2 (see Powers of 2).

For computers, the Greek prefixes for numbers were changed to powers of 2, as in the following table:

Prefix	Number
Kilo	1,024
Mega	1,048,576
Giga	1,073,741,824
Tera	1,099,511,627,776

So this guy we mentioned in the beginning, who said his computer has 2 gigabytes of memory, meant he has 2,147,483,648 bytes (two times 1,073,741,824). This is a little more than two billion bytes. Each byte is eight bits (see entry), so he can store in his computer's memory 17,179,869,184 bits.

By the way, one of the largest numbers that has its own name is the number "googol" (10^{100}), which is 1 followed by one hundred zeroes (meaning 1,000,000,000... and another 91 zeroes). Writing it is hard, but not when you compare it to the number "googolplex": 1 followed by googol zeroes. Scientists claim that even if we took all the stars in the universe and turned them into ink and paper, we still wouldn't have enough to write this number.

Malware

Most software programs are written in order to help people. However, there is also malware, malicious software, deliberately written to cause damage. Would you go into a computer store and ask for malware? Would you be willing to pay for it? If someone offered you malware for free, would you take it? Of course not! No one wants malware!

Therefore, malware must be sneaky. It must come uninvited and infiltrate a computer unnoticed, or in disguise. Different types of malware use different kinds of nasty tricks. Here are two examples.

Computer viruses: a computer virus is a software program that attaches itself to "good" software. It hides inside the good software, and no one knows it's there. When the user activates the "good" software, he or she unknowingly activates the virus as well. From the moment the virus is activated, it starts searching for other software and attaches a copy of itself to them as well. No wonder they're called viruses: they spread like a contagious disease, with one "sick" program infecting all those around it. In this way, computer viruses can spread around the globe in days, causing huge damage.

Computer worms: unlike viruses, worms transmit themselves through the Internet and don't need to attach themselves to other programs. Here's an example of a real computer worm that spread in the year 2000. This worm was called "I-Love-You" and this is how it worked. An innocent user received an email titled "I-Love-You." He opened it immediately, of course; everybody is curious about love letters. The email contained a file that looked like a love letter, but it was no letter. It was the worm! When the user opened it, he actually activated the worm. The worm's actions from this point were simple and clever: it searched for all email addresses listed in this user's address list and sent a copy of itself to every one of them. If this user had forty friends, all of them now got this fake "I-Love-You" letter. Of course those people, too, were immediately curious to read a love letter, opened it, and sent the worm to their friends as well, and so on. A worm can multiply this way so quickly that whole sections of the Internet may become clogged with millions of worms.

Worms, viruses, and other types of malware cause enormous damage to businesses and personal computers. Their creators, if they are caught, are brought to trial and severely punished.

Megabyte

See Large Numbers

Operating System

The operating system is a computer program in charge of managing the computer. In a typical personal computer, the operating system is usually Microsoft Windows.

Port

Let's say you want to call your friend, and let's say his name is Tom, and you don't have his cell phone number, only his home number. Since Tom doesn't live alone, it is possible someone else will pick up the phone—Tom's mother, for example. In this case you would say to her something like this: "Can I please talk to Tom?"

In the Internet (see entry), each computer is identified by an IP address (see entry), which acts as its phone number. You can send a message to a distant computer if you know its IP address. But the computer is "home" to many applications: an email client, a web browser, chat applications, games, media players, and possibly many more. Therefore, the IP address alone is not enough: you need to specify to which particular application you want to "talk."

This is what port numbers are for. Each type of application has its own port number. For example, email services are associated with port numbers 25, 143, and 110 (each has a slightly different role). So, for example, if you want to send an email to a computer whose IP address is 100.90.80.70, you need to write on the outgoing message that it is destined to IP address 100.90.80.70 and port number 25. (Don't worry: the e-mail client running on your computer handles these tedious tasks for you.)

Another widely used port number is 80. It is used to access web sites. When you surf to any of the popular sites, for example, www.wikipedia.org, what happens is as follows: First your computer looks up the IP address of www.wikipedia.org (*see* IP address). Let's say it finds it to be 10.20.30.40. Then your computer sends a message to 10.20.30.40, port number 80, asking for the content of the web site. In response it gets the home page of Wikipedia.

Port 80

See Port

Powers of Two

Imagine you read in the newspaper that 10,000 people came to see a rock concert. Surely this isn't the exact number. The real number is more likely something like 9,973 or 10,213. However, since people don't like complicated numbers, they usually round them to simpler numbers, like 10,000.

We are used to the decimal numeral system (*see* Decimal and Binary Numeral System) and therefore, what we call round numbers are powers of 10, that is, the result of multiplying the number ten with itself. For example, the number 10,000 is the result of 10 x 10 x 10 x 10 ("ten to the power of four" or, in short: 10^4).

Computers use the binary numeral system, in which there are only two digits. In this system, numbers that are considered round are powers of two, the result of multiplying two by itself several times. For example, the number 8 is considered a round number because it is a power of two: 2 x 2 x 2 = 8 (or 2^3). If you write the number 8 in binary representation you'll discover that it really does look round. It's written like this: 1000.

The number 256 is also a power of two: 2^8 (2 x 2 x 2 x 2 x 2 x 2 x 2 x 2 = 256).

Since powers of two are considered round, you will frequently come across them when dealing with a computer-related subject. For example, a USB flash drive (memory stick, disk on key), usually comes with a capacity of 4, 8, or 16 gigabytes (*see* Large Numbers); all three numbers are powers of two. It would be quite rare to find a USB flash drive with a capacity of 5 or 11 gigabytes.

In this book as well, you'll find many powers of two. Actually, if you read the whole story carefully, you'll find all the powers of two up to 4,096, that is: 1, 2, 4, 8, 16, 32, 64, 128, 256, 512, 1024, 2048, and 4096.

Worm

See Malware

26788330R00099

Made in the USA
Lexington, KY
15 October 2013